Amanda Minnie Douglas

Kathie's Harvest Days

Amanda Minnie Douglas

Kathie's Harvest Days

ISBN/EAN: 9783337384692

Printed in Europe, USA, Canada, Australia, Japan

Cover: Foto ©Andreas Hilbeck / pixelio.de

More available books at **www.hansebooks.com**

KATHIE'S HARVEST DAYS

BY

AMANDA M. DOUGLAS

AUTHOR OF "HELEN GRANT BOOKS," "LITTLE RED
HOUSE SERIES," ETC.

FRONTISPIECE BY C. HOWARD

BOSTON
LOTHROP, LEE & SHEPARD CO.

ALICE MAUD BUCK.

So let thy life, dear child, in its young dawning,
   Unfold with blossoms fragrant, rare, and sweet,
Like clustered lilies on an Easter morning,
   Faith, love, and patience making all complete.

WOODSIDE, 1871.

CONTENTS.

CHAPTER VIII.

CHAPTER IX.

CHAPTER X.

CHAPTER XI.

CHAPTER XII.

CHAPTER XIII.

CHAPTER XIV.

KATHIE'S HARVEST DAYS.

CHAPTER I.

A SHADOW WITH THE SUNSHINE.

THE household was gathered in the cosey sitting-room at Cedarwood. Uncle Robert was reading aloud while the ladies sewed. And though the history had its charm for Kathie, still her mind wandered now and then, as she glanced at Aunt Ruth. In a fortnight she was to go away, — dear Aunt Ruth, who had been connected with all her life, farther back even than she could remember. And somehow it seemed as if she could not be quite reconciled to the fact.

Uncle Robert closed his book and glanced at her, studying the thoughtful face for a moment. Every day was taking her a little beyond the glad, rippling shore of childhood to the deeper waters. Just as he was about to speak the bell rang, and a familiar voice startled them.

"Why, Meredith!" he exclaimed, "you are the last person I expected to see to-night. When did you return?"

"About noon. I should have brought Jessie over with me, but she was too tired; so she wished to be remembered to all. How lovely you look here! Miss Conover, you grow younger every day."

Aunt Ruth smiled, while a soft color flushed her cheek.

"Your brother — " began Uncle Robert, and then he paused.

"It is bad enough, — the very worst. Poor George! I feel sorry that so great a misfortune should come upon him, and yet it seems the natural result of such unbounded extravagance. You should have heard Dr. Markham on the subject"; and Mr. Meredith smiled in spite of his sadness.

"Is it a total loss?"

"A clean sweep, as one may say. He has given up everything to his creditors, but that will not cover all. They propose to release him at present, though, and give him a fair chance."

"I am glad of that."

"Yes. George is honorable, and will pay to the

uttermost farthing as he is prospered. It has changed all my plans, however. We shall not go abroad."

"Oh!" Kathie uttered, sympathetically. She and Jessie had talked over this tour to Europe until both had become actually in love with it. London and Paris for the winter, an Easter in Rome, and a summer among the Alps and the lakes.

"It was a great disappointment to Jessie, but she gave it up bravely. We shall try it some other time. Who knows but you may make one of the party then, Kathie?"

"I can hardly believe in anything quite so delightful," she answered.

"Since it appears possible for George to retrieve the past in some degree, I feel it my duty to do all in my power. So we have taken a house in New York, where Jessie and I expect to set up our Penates, — is that right, Kathie? — and I purpose to become a business man straightway."

Mr. Meredith laughed as he uttered this, yet it was not quite the old joyous sound.

"I am very thankful that my health is so firmly re-established," he continued. "And I have had a small taste of work, consequently it will not be altogether strange to me."

Kathie knew well to what work he referred. **He** had been Rob's hero in the old time for his gay humor and careless indifference, but it seemed to her that every year brought him up to some better, grander height.

" I am very sorry for the changes it must make in your brother's family," Mrs. Alston said.

Mr. Meredith shrugged his shoulders. " The lesson does not come a bit too soon to George's wife," he said, in a peculiar tone. " Indeed, if she had listened to him, part of this might have been averted. She could not believe there was any necessity for retrenchment, and her summer campaign was the height of folly. Jessie and I are particularly thankful that we were not induced to join it."

" Poor Ada ! " Kathie exclaimed, involuntarily.

" She will have an opportunity to come to her senses before she has gone too far astray, I hope," Mr. Meredith said, a little sternly.

" And yet it will make a sad and great change," was Aunt Ruth's comment, in the softest of voices. " We have lived through one such episode ourselves."

" Not quite," Mr. Meredith returned, warmly. " I do not believe that you had yourself to blame for

extravagance and folly, and the social sins that eat
the heart out of home like a canker-worm. George
was unusually prosperous during the war, and his
wife thought there never could be any end to money.
It may be a bitter experience, but none the less
wholesome. And I think Ada was in a fair way of
being ruined. There are enough shallow, heartless
girls for the next generation of wives, without her
adding to the list."

" What will they do ? " asked Kathie.

" They have given up both the country-house and
that in New York, and must of course live very quietly. There is to be an auction sale of the furniture
that they will not need, for George is determined to
pay his way as far as possible, and I honor him for
it. So you need not be afraid of Ada's grandeur
hereafter, Kathie."

The child made no immediate reply. There had
been many times when Ada had not hesitated to display the advantages of what she considered her supe-
rior station and wealth, and had wounded Kathie's
tender heart in different ways, but she was generous
and forgot this now. She could only think how hard
it would be for Ada to relinquish her luxuries, her

aims, and her pleasures, since her whole life last
summer seemed to be centred in them.

What if she had to give up this beautiful Cedarwood, the luxuriant grounds and lovely flowers, the
pleasant, cosey house, with its pictures, books, and
pretty furniture, and go back to the little cottage
where Uncle Robert found her! Ada would not be-
quite as poor as that, neither had she all of Ada's ele-
gances now, so the change would be nearly as great.

Uncle Robert and Mr. Meredith plunged into a
business talk that she hardly cared to follow, so she
kept studying the fire blazing so cheerfully in the
grate, and thinking her own thoughts. Now and
then her mother's voice made a pleasant break in
the earnest conversation, but, having discussed the
few important points, Mr. Meredith rose to leave
presently.

" Be sure you come over to see Jessie to-morrow,"
he said. " She will be packing and fussing after the
fashion of a hen with one chick, a pet indulgence
among you women "; and he pinched Kathie's rosy
cheek, contrasting her in his mind with pale, hysteri-
cal Ada, whose thin face and sunken eyes gave her a
ghostly look. Uncle Robert started to walk part of

the way with him, and Mrs. Alston went to the kitchen to give Hannah a few orders.

"Is n't it very, very sad, Aunt Ruth, in spite of —" There Kathie stopped. She meant in spite of the sense of justice or right, or even punishment, that might possibly be construed into this misfortune.

"Yes, my dear. I am glad that your strongest feeling is one of sympathy."

"O Aunt Ruth, you don't think I *could* be glad for the loss and the change and the sorrow !"

"I am thankful that you cannot be "; and Aunt Ruth smiled tenderly into Kathie's eyes. "It is a sign of a narrow, selfish mind when one person takes delight in another's misfortunes. And though Ada has been fond of making the very best of her position and her wealth, and perhaps not always displayed the kindest regard for another's feelings, that is no reason why you should indulge in a petty and unkind spirit."

"I should not like to be poor again. Do you suppose that we ever — shall — "

"No one is ever quite safe from losses," Aunt Ruth said, filling Kathie's long pause.

"Yet I am afraid that I am still a little selfish."

she returned, with a faint half-smile. "What do you suppose I was thinking about when Mr. Meredith came in ?"

Aunt Ruth questioned her with an arch look.

"That you were all going to have a nice time; you and General Mackenzie in Washington, and Jessie and Mr. Meredith in Europe, while I should have only school and music practices."

"*Only ?*" Aunt Ruth uttered this with a peculiar intonation.

"It was very forgetful, ungrateful almost. And yet there is a puzzle in it all. We are constantly longing for the things we cannot have, and sometimes do not really appreciate or care for the things that we might enjoy. I can't seem to understand just where the wrong is."

"My darling, when anything sweet and dear is taken out of our lives, even for a little while, we cannot help but miss it. That is a part of our nature, and God never designed that we should thrust aside all tender feeling. The wrong is when we fret and make ourselves discontented over the many blessings left us. You would have mamma and Uncle Robert, and the duties that every day brings."

"And then I thought how noble it was for Mr. Meredith and Jessie to give up their pleasure for such a purpose. It is as heroic as his going out with the army."

"Still higher in one respect. He had to deny, not only himself, but the wife he loved dearly, and to make himself content with business, which he does not greatly admire. Few brothers would have done it. This is a little of the good fruit, Kathie, which we are to bring forth in the vineyard where we are set to labor."

"I begin to understand," Kathie said, slowly.

"And you see it is the work of a whole life. We are not to be discouraged when we fail, but to turn to Him who has promised strength, who has said 'Abide in me.'"

"I shall miss you very much when you are gone, Aunt Ruth. It will seem so strange. And yet I shall be very glad to have you and General Mackenzie happy."

Aunt Ruth colored with a touch of girlishness. "It seems odd to have a separate happiness of my own," she made answer, "and I can't help believing that it came partly through you."

"Then I must be quite content with it. And I am most glad, Aunt Ruth, that Bruce is so happy over it. So you will have a grown-up son. Do you suppose he will call you mother?"

Kathie's face turned scarlet as she realized the force of the question.

"That is as he likes, dear. I want always to be a good and tender friend to him, and never make him feel that I have unduly thrust myself into a place that must always have a peculiar sacredness to him."

"Aunt Ruth," she said, after a long silence, "is n't it a little strange that some of the happiness that comes into one person's life seems to be taken out of another's? Is there not enough to go all round?"

"It is God's way of making us share our joys and blessings with one another, and to keep us from becoming selfish. If his love was great enough to take us all in, shall not ours, in copying that, go out to those around us?"

"Yes," she answered, softly.

Aunt Ruth began to gather up her sewing, and Kathie put the books in their places. Then Uncle Robert returned, and they had to talk a little about the matter that interested them so deeply.

" Mr. Meredith had no idea that it was so positively hopeless until he went down.   His brother feels very much disheartened, and that is one reason Edward wishes to remain.   Besides, he could not put his money in the business and travel in the manner that he desires.   It is very sweet in Jessie to give up her pleasures so willingly.   Last summer Mrs. Meredith believed all the favors and benefits to be within her power, and perhaps had Jessie taken instructions of her worldly wisdom she would hardly have been as generous now."

"It is getting late and you must run off to bed, Kathie," said her mother.

The next afternoon Kathie paid her friend a visit. Jessie had been spending nearly a month in New York, and the letters had been chatty epistles of pictures and concerts and small tea-drinkings, rather than the more serious matters of life.   So there was a great deal to tell.

" It was all Edward's goodness," declared Jessie.   "At first I felt as if I really could not make the sacrifice. Mrs. Meredith treated me last summer as if I was a kind of underbred interloper in the family, of whom she felt almost ashamed " ; and Jessie colored warmly. "I am so glad that I did not go to Saratoga with them, and the seaside did Edward so much good. But when he came to explain the matter, and I saw what a point of conscience it was with him, I yielded at once."

"I am so sorry that you had to give up the pleasure."

"It may come by and by. He really shamed me by his nobleness, Kathie, and I know, too, that he does n't like the confinement and routine of business. And I could not help pitying Mrs. Meredith and Ada, they are so utterly heart-broken and despairing. The auction is to be this week, and I felt that I could not stay to witness their sorrow. It is very hard to give up that elegant house with all its luxuries. I think it would pain any one, so I do not blame their grief at parting with it."

"Poor Ada!"

"Poor foolish Ada! Her head has been so filled with the frivolities of fashionable life, and turned by the admiration she has received, that she is blindly unreasonable and helpless. O Kathie, be thankful that your mother has better sense!"

"What are they going to do?"

" Board for a few weeks until they can suit themselves. Edward advised that they should take a
house immediately, and proposed the one next to
ours, but Mrs. Meredith thought it altogether too
small. It will be very pleasant and pretty, Kathie,
and I must confess that it looks quite grand to me ";
and Jessie laughed. " I shall expect a visit from you
during the holidays."

" And I shall be delighted to come. I have not
been to New York since the winter with Aunt Ruth."

" How odd that Aunt Ruth is to be married! I
like General Mackenzie so much. But you should
have seen Dr. Markham when Edward told him.
'Did n't I predict that she would be dancing on
the green one of these days?' said he; 'and here
she has carried off the very man that half the women
I know have been setting their caps for these dozen
years or more.' And then he went on with that
touch of sweet gravity which comes now and then in
his voice: 'But, after all, little Kathie was the best
doctor among us. I don't believe I could have
brought her through but for the child.'"

The tears of tender remembrance shone on the
drooping lashes hiding Kathie's eyes.

"It seems to me as if everybody put something sweet and pleasant into my life," she said, softly.

"Because you are always doing it as well"; and Jessie looked up with a bright, answering smile. "That is the grand secret of life. I don't wonder it is called the 'Golden Rule.' And you do try earnestly, I know."

"And fail often," was the low, humble reply.

"We all do. I suppose if we did not we should get too proud and self-reliant, and stray away from our loving Shepherd. But, after we have wandered, it is so good to get back to his strong arms."

Kathie was thinking it over in her simple child's fashion, that always made anything so real to her.

"When is Aunt Ruth to be married?" Jessie asked, presently.

"In about a fortnight."

"How oddly events come about! Only the other day I was a girl like you, and Charlie a little boy; and here you will soon be a woman, marrying like the rest of us, I dare say. But Aunt Ruth's is like a romance, — a May after the summer is ended. And that *I* should never suspect, though Edward declares he did. What are you going to do without her ? "

" I don't know. I feel a little selfish sometimes, only General Mackenzie is so — so — "

" Splendid ! " declared Jessie, laughing. " Why can't we use the word once in a while ? You will miss her so much ! "

Ah ! Kathie knew that, and her heart had ached more than once.

" Now I must tell you about my house. It is only a short distance from the park, not very large, they all say ; but I don't know how I am to live every-where in it. We are going to furnish very simply, for Edward thinks we shall go abroad in three years at the latest, but it will be fresh and pretty and home-like. Yet it seems queer to think of *my* keeping a house."

" Does it ? " and Kathie smiled oddly.

" I used to think, that, when I was married, I should go directly to a home of my own and settle down at once. It was not to be very far from here, where Charlie would run in every day, father and mother come to tea once a week, and grandmother stay a month at a time and knit stockings for my husband

Instead, I have been picnicking round in hotels and hospitals and sea-sides until I almost wonder if I be I."

Kathie laughed heartily at that.

"But now we shall be old-fashioned orthodox people. I hope everybody will pay us a visit. We shall have a guest-chamber always ready, and I will do my best at the small, sweet courtesies of life. We are to begin with one servant, and I wish it was not necessary to have any. I should like to try my skill for a little while ; but it would be dreadfully unfashionable, and ruin the softness of my hands."

"Which would be sad indeed," declared Mr. Meredith, entering. "How much have you packed since dinner ? "

"I am all through for the present. To-morrow will finish."

"I ought to go back in the morning, if you do not mind being left here for a few days. Kathie, will you keep her safely ? "

"I should like to have her to keep," Kathie retorted. "I want some one to take Aunt Ruth's place."

"But what would I do for good and all ? — as the children say."

"You are not likely to lose me very long at a time," was Jessie's rejoinder.

Mr. Meredith drew Kathie on the sofa beside him, while Jessie brushed her tumbled hair, and they had a sweet, half-sad talk concerning the changes that were to be.

"And how is Rob?" he asked, directly. "I can't tell you how I want to see him."

"He is very well, and doing remarkably in his studies, Uncle Robert thinks. I do believe he is more in earnest than ever before."

"I predict that Rob comes out all right in the end, like the prince in the fairy story. You see, Kathie, it *is* hard work for boys to be good. But the key-note of Rob's heart has been touched."

She knew what he meant by the peculiar light in his eyes.

"I never can bear to hear Rob blamed altogether for that," she returned, softly. "It *was* a good deal my fault."

"But we were so thankful to have you alive once more, that we never had the heart to scold you," he answered, gayly.

The tea-bell rang at that moment, and they both

insisted that Kathie should stay, promising to accompany her home afterward.

"The child grows dearer and sweeter every day," said Grandmother Darrell, after she had kissed her "good-night."

CHAPTER II.

AUNT RUTH'S NEW LIFE.

THERE was a quiet wedding at Cedarwood one sunshiny November day. Rob came home from school as a special privilege. A few choice friends were gathered in the spacious parlor, that was fragrant and beautiful with flowers. Kathie had arranged them. Not any great stately pyramids, but slender vases filled with the rarest, and small mounds of dainty loveliness covering the dishes whereon they were gracefully strewn. For the perfume and bright freshness it might have been a midsummer day. And with some of the taller house-plants and long trails of ground-pine Uncle Robert had arranged a sort of arch where Aunt Ruth was to stand.

She came down quietly, after the guests were assembled, in her soft gray silk, that did not rustle, but fell about her in clinging folds. There was the faintest flush on her cheek, that gave her a touch of lingering girlishness. Was it the patient grace of affection that had kept her so young? There had been many hard, dreary years to live through, yet some very bright sunshine had come at last.

General Mackenzie looked very brave and noble in his military dress, and that peculiar tender refinement in his face that had come from the practice of the higher virtues, rather than worldly polish, — a Christian gentleman, who had sought first the kingdom of heaven, and then had all other things added to him. He listened and responded reverentially, and took the proffered hand in his with the sweetness and faith of a great love. And, after the last words had been uttered, he stooped and kissed her.

"I never saw anything more solemnly beautiful in my life," Jessie said. "I could hardly keep the tears from coming into my eyes, and I thought all the time that it was just as much a marriage in heaven as here upon earth."

"Aunt Ruth deserves every bit of happiness," declared Rob. "And I am glad there is so much style about it, that he is a general, and that they are going to Washington. I would like to give one rousing hurrah!"

Kathie smiled in spite of herself.

There was a refreshment table in the dining-room, and after the congratulations the company went out. Aunt Ruth cut the cake and received the good wishes in her lady-like manner. Then she went up stairs to put on her bonnet and gloves.

"My dear niece Kathie," the General said, "how little we could have thought of this, the night so long ago when I first met you! Yet a charm in your sweet child's face attracted me involuntarily. And now, if I have taken something precious out of your life, I hope to be able to place fresh blessings in it. You are so generous with all of yours."

Kathie's lip quivered and her voice failed when she would have spoken. But she understood how it was, and how these exchanges were going on all over the world, every one bringing the soul nearer to the great brotherhood of angels above, who give continually, asking nothing back.

"So, for the present, your loss is my gain, but some day I will share my joys with you as a member of your happy household. We shall not forget you for an hour."

Kathie smiled her thanks for the cordial tone, but she confessed to Jessie afterward that she felt very

much like crying. "I did n't suppose weddings could
be so sad," she said.

Quite a party went to the station. General Mackenzie was going directly to West Point to give
Bruce a sight of his new mother, and thence to
Washington, where business would occupy him for
the next six weeks. Jessie and Mr. Meredith had
their house settled to their liking, and were to return
immediately. Rob begged hard to stay until the next
morning, to have a chance to see some of the boys.
"Because I am going to study up, and not lose a
single recitation. I promised Dr. Goldthwaite."

They did not see much of him until bed-time.
Kathie had a quiet evening with mamma and Uncle
Robert, for Freddy had supplied himself so bounti-
fully with luxuries that he had gone to bed with a
headache and no supper.

The event made quite a stir in Brookside, it must
be confessed.

"I wonder what the Haddens would say to that!"
exclaimed Sue Coleman. "Kathie Alston certainly
has the most elegant friends and connections of any
girl I know. I should not wonder if she went to
Europe some day, and eclipsed us all."

Mrs. George Meredith was as much astonished as anybody.

"The idea of such a man marrying a woman who is lame, and not particularly handsome, nor rich, nor young! Why, he might have had almost any one in our set. He is so fine-looking and cultivated, and has such a nice position. It is a shame for him to throw himself away!"

So had she bewailed her brother-in-law's marriage; and yet she could not help admitting in her secret heart that hardly one among her fashionable friends would have been as sweet and generous as Jessie. She was learning by bitter and humiliating experience that those who had flattered and caressed her in the midst of opulence would not turn out of their way now to give her a kind word or a moment's pleasure.

Mr. Meredith had been a most indulgent husband. During their prosperity he had allowed his wife to indulge her expensive tastes lavishly. But he was a man of sound principles and strict integrity where business was concerned. He had not looked for his brother to come forward so nobly and help him regain his lost position, but, now that opportunity

offered, he meant to use the utmost energy in en-
deavoring to retrieve the past. He would allow himself and his family no needless indulgence that might
tend to jeopardize another's fortune.

Mrs. Meredith thought this extremely hard. Her
husband's position among men was nearly the same
as heretofore; indeed, his manly course had brought
him warmer, truer friends. After a few years of retrenchment he might find himself on a firm basis,
once more a prosperous man. But it seemed as if
she was compelled to give up everything. She had
pleaded for a grander house than the one he proposed.

" My dear wife," he said, " we cannot afford it. We
must practice the strictest economy for some time to
come. I will not risk Edward's money, since he has
been so generous for my sake. I have fixed the utmost limit for our expenses this year, and we must
not exceed it."

" But it is so cruel now, when Ada was just beginning to go into society. It ruins her chances for
everything. By the time we can attain to any style
she will be faded, unattractive, and past youth. No
one will want to marry her."

" It seems that some one wanted to marry Miss

Conover," he returned. "If Ada can do as well as that when she is past thirty, I shall be satisfied."

Ada bemoaned the state of affairs no less bitterly. And when, at last, they did decide upon an inconvenient, cheaply built house, whose greatest recommendation was a rather stylish neighborhood, and began to settle themselves, the task seemed harder and more hopeless than ever. The tidy, practised French nurse had been superseded by a young girl at less than half the wages, while the kitchen was given over to a very ordinary cook. The younger children grew untidy and disorderly, the meals were served in a careless fashion, instead of the once neat and elegant manner.

"But what *can* one do!" Mrs. Meredith would exclaim. "Cheap servants, like cheap furniture, never are worth the having. If your father *could* see this, Ada; but he is like other men. He can understand nothing outside of his business. And how we are to live on such a mere pittance puzzles me!"

Ada did n't think it her place to dust the parlor or replace the scattered articles, or to look after the children. George and Willie were sent to school, and

3

soon became insufferably noisy. Florence, missing the steady hand that had amused and governed, and growing tired of the lonesome nursery, fretted every one out of patience. Mary let the steam of washing and cooking get through the house, the fires were always going out, and the place was as comfortless as one could well imagine.

Now and then Mrs. Meredith roused herself and made a spasmodic effort, but the task appeared so hopeless! "There was nothing to do with," she declared continually. Ada practised her music a little, lounged in her own room, and, having no other resource, eagerly devoured novels of all kinds, or took a languid walk, to be slighted and wounded by a cold recognition from some bygone friend, whom she bewailed, in her solitude, with tears.

Jessie tried to rouse her from her depression, but Ada met all her efforts with cold indifference. She invited her to dinners or suppers with a few pleasant guests, but even here she would not make herself agreeable. "It was not what she had been used to. Aunt Jessie was well enough in her way, but —"

And so all the wide, rich, beautiful life beyond, teeming with love and duty, springs and seedtimes,

summers and fruits, golden autumns and gracious
harvest fields, were shut out.   No pure, breezy, fresh-
ening air to stir and quicken her soul, no tender
thoughts for her irritable heart and brain, no kindly
deeds for her listless hands.

But not so with Kathie.   There was the "next" to
her, the new duty in the place of the old one finished,
or slipped out, or gone into other hands.   Her circle
was continually widening, her lines of sympathy
reached out hither and thither and found something
to draw in or cling to.   It was a little lonesome at
first, and once in a while, when she lay on the crimson lounge in Aunt Ruth's room, after the lessons
and reading were finished, she could n't help having
a quiet little cry over the places where a smile had
vanished and a tender voice was heard no more.   She
was very easily touched to the heart, for all her
cheerful ways.

So at home she began to take up Freddy, who,
like all the rest of the world, seemed growing apace;
growing out of playthings into books, growing out of
baby inconsequence into thought and wonder and
gleams of shrewd wisdom.   He had little of Rob's
boisterous spirit of fun and careless indifference, and

none of his touchy pride in being "fond of the girls."

Kathie gave him some simple music lessons and taught him to sing with her. She let him drive the pony-carriage, and Uncle Robert had taught him to ride Jasper.

At school the circle widened as well. She was getting over her shyness somewhat. The elder girls found her a very charming companion, and they began to think no party complete without her. Perhaps the great thing was that she never carried an obtrusive self about with her. She did not aim for the high places, the prettiest characters in tableaux, or the brightest parts in charades, and yet, when everybody else was satisfied, there was always some particular thing that every one insisted she could do better than the others.

"Do you know how very near it is to Christmas, Uncle Robert?" she asked, one afternoon. "What are we going to do?"

"I wonder what you would like best of all?"

She placed her books on the convenient shelf, and hung up her hat.

"I don't know, I have had so many things. You remember what Mr. Meredith said in his letter?"

"Well, shall we go and keep Christmas with them ?"

There was something in Uncle Robert's face that mystified her, — the least little touch of amusement that she could not quite understand.

" O, they are coming here !" she exclaimed.

" No. Guess again."

" Aunt Ruth will be home, then."

" Not quite that, either."

" Well, I am sure I cannot tell, then."

" We had letters to-day. Here is yours. Perhaps it may give you a new idea for Christmas."

She read it eagerly. A long, sweet epistle from Aunt Ruth, and a postscript from the General.

" Oh !" she exclaimed. " If I really could ! If you would n't feel lonesome. And then to have them come back with me !"

" It will be very pleasant for you. General Mackenzie will return on the third of January, spending some three or four days in New York, so you will have a chance to see Jessie and Mr. Meredith."

" It is altogether enchanting, like the things that used to happen when I half believed in fairies. But can I really go ?"

"Your mother thinks so. It will keep you out of school for a week, but you must study the harder afterward. And it is such an excellent opportunity."

"I don't know what to say. Where is mamma?"

"She went out with Mrs. Grayson to visit a family in great distress."

It seemed to Kathie as if there ought not to be any pain or sorrow in the world when she was so entirely happy. Then she had to read her letter over again. Only six weeks since Aunt Ruth was married, and yet it appeared half a lifetime. And to go to Washington! to see the Capitol, the great mansions, the President himself, perhaps. Oh! was n't it the least little bit of a dream?

A friend of the General would escort Kathie from Jersey City, if it was inconvenient for Uncle Robert to take the journey. He was to leave on the morning of the twenty-third, and would meet them at the depot or the hotel where he was staying. So, if Kathie would write back immediately, the matter could be put in train at once.

They made all arrangements that evening, and she wrote her letter in a most delightful mood.

"I declare it is too bad!" said one of the girls the

next day. "Here we are going to have a Christmas
fair and two surprise-parties, and charades at Hattie
Norman's. How are we to get along without you ?"

Kathie glanced up and met Emma Lauriston's eyes.
Both remembered a time when they were quite elated
in the prospect of "getting along" without her. But
Kathie's sunny nature held no grudges. She was
only too glad to be good friends with all the girls, to
bring her gifts, if she had any, to bear upon the little
every-day living which, after all, is the great wheel
that turns the world.

"Everything lovely does come to you, but I am
sure you deserve it," Emma whispered, softly.

"I wonder if you will go to any receptions ? and,
oh ! what will you wear ?"

Kathie laughed.

"I suppose I shall see everything that can be seen
in that brief while" ; but she could n't help thinking
that the dearest sight of all would be Aunt Ruth.

It required some courage to keep strictly to the
lessons after that. Bruce wrote her a letter in which
he said he did not envy any one in the world, but he
thought he would just as lief be Kathie Alston for
ten or twelve days, beginning at Christmas, as a
great overgrown boy at a military academy.

He had accepted and liked his new mother very cordially. Of his own he had a very slight remembrance, and to boys without homes or mothers a gentle, considerate love like this is very tender and sweet.

"It is too bad that he cannot go as well," Kathie said to Uncle Robert. "I have so many nice times that I do begin to feel conscience smitten when I think of all who are crowded out."

So, at last, Kathie's small trunk was packed and directed, and Uncle Robert took her down to the city. As she had to start early, he decided that it would be better for them to stay at the hotel, for convenience in the morning. So they hunted up Mr. Winterdyne, and found him a very pleasant, agreeable gentleman, past forty. He had seen General Mackenzie and his wife only the week before, and had heard all about this little niece, and would be very glad to take charge of her during the rather tiresome journey.

She was up betimes, as fresh and sweet as a rose. The morning was cold and gray, so her happy face was like a gleam of sunshine. Uncle Robert said good-by at the gateway, and Mr. Winterdyne

drew her arm through his, quite as if she had been a
young lady. He seated her carefully near the window, hung up his satchel and umbrella, chatting
pleasantly so that she might not feel strange. And
then they steamed slowly out of the depot and were
on their way.

"We shall have a storm before noon, I think,"
Mr. Winterdyne said, presently. "It threatens
snow."

"Do you suppose it will delay us?" Kathie asked.
Now that she had started she could think only of the
journey's end.

"O no, I guess not. The weather may moderate,
and in that case it is more likely to be rain, as we go
farther south."

He talked to Kathie quite a while, naming the
towns they passed and giving bits of their history.
Then two gentlemen came through the car and engaged him in a business conversation.

"Your daughter, Winterdyne?" asked one of them.

"No. General Mackenzie's niece. I am taking
her to Washington. Miss Alston."

Kathie gave a timid little bow to the pleasant eyes
that smiled upon her.

"Have you ever been in Washington before?" he asked.

Kathie answered in the negative.

"Quite commonplace again, eh, Winterdyne? The camps and barracks and armies have vanished. We can hardly believe now that we have lived through such a terrible struggle. But many a brave fellow never came back again. Romances and tragedies were common in those days."

"Yes."

"Did you ever know Ned Meredith?"

"I think not."

Kathie started in quick surprise at the name.

"The poor fellow had a hard time of it, — was wounded and barely lived. A right pretty girl came on and married him, and I guess that pulled him through as much as anything. I took dinner with them a few days ago, and they are as happy as bees in clover. There were some brave little women as well. So you have a taste for romances?" and he smiled over at Kathie again.

"It was all reality to me, — to us," she said. "My uncle was there at the time, and Mrs. Meredith is a very dear friend."

"Oh !" and he studied her again. " I think I remember you by a picture. Is n't it Kathie Alston? and was not your uncle a Mr. Conover? Why, I feel quite well acquainted.

Kathie listened to the story of the marriage again, and some incidents of coolness and bravery on Mr. Meredith's part that somehow touched her heart and made her feel prouder than ever of him.

At Trenton the new friends shook hands and parted.

" It is beginning to snow," said Mr. Winterdyne. " Are you comfortable? would you like to look over any of these books ?"

Presently they reached Philadelphia, and Kathie was very much interested in the strange sights. Mr. Winterdyne took her out on the platform a few moments, for a little rest and a breath of fresh air, he said. Then they whirled on and on again, but the snow seemed to gain and the wind blew it in eddying gusts. It spoiled the prospect, as they could see nothing beyond dim outlines.

Kathie read a little, for she did not wish to annoy her kind escort by claiming too much of his attention. The motion of the cars and the silence made her quite drowsy, and she could not help nodding.

It was rather late when they reached their destination, owing to the unavoidable delay of the storm. Kathie felt somewhat frightened amid the din and hurry and strange faces that stared at her at every turn. Mr. Winterdyne pushed his way through the crowd, anxiously looking for his friend.

"Ah, here you are!" exclaimed a familiar voice. "My dear Kathie!"

The clasp and the smile were so fervent that they at once restored her spirits, for she was beginning to feel homesick. General Mackenzie drew her close with sheltering tenderness.

"I have a carriage in waiting. Won't you come home with us, Winterdyne, and take a cup of tea? I am more than obliged for all your kindness. It has been a dreary day for a journey."

"Thank you, but I am late now to meet an engagement. Miss Kathie proved a very agreeable travelling companion, and I am happy to have done you ever so slight a service. Good night. I expect to see you both again."

They soon rattled homeward. It was so delightful to be in a warm, cheerful room and have dear Aunt Ruth's kisses of welcome, to slip out of her water-

proof and lay aside her hat. She felt stiff and
cramped, to be sure, but a few hours would rest
her, and by morning she would be her olden self.

It seemed, somehow, as if Aunt Ruth had changed.
She was quite a stately lady, indeed, and looked very
stylish in her black silk that trailed around her slender figure, and the soft lace at her neck and wrists.
But the dear face was as sweet as ever.

"O Aunt Ruth," Kathie exclaimed, "have you been
very, very happy? You look so."

"Of course she has, my little girl. Did you think
an old gray-beard like me had lost the art of making people satisfied and content? Why, I dare say I
shall charm you so that you will never want to go
back to Cedarwood. You don't half know how dangerous I am."

Kathie laughed genially. How proud Aunt Ruth
must be of him, so manly and tender, and to have
him all for her own!

"But you must not be starved, little Kathie," he
said, ringing the bell. "Railroad fare is not the most
satisfactory of all feasting. We will have a cosey
little tea to ourselves."

Aunt Ruth emptied the side-table and spread a

snowy cloth over it. In a few moments the servant entered with a tray and arranged a dainty meal. Aunt Ruth poured the tea, and the General tempted Kathie with every delicacy, taking a taste himself to assure her that it was as good as it looked. They talked of the dear ones at Cedarwood, of letters and pleasures and kind remembrances, until Kathie began to feel weary and sleepy.

Aunt Ruth had to make her a bed in the sitting-room, but the sofa was roomy, and fenced in with chairs to keep the blankets from slipping.

"I thought you would feel more at home here with me in the next room, than in one of the distant chambers by yourself."

"I should n't want to go very far from you in this strange country," said Kathie, with her good-night kiss.

CHAPTER III.

HOLIDAY JOYS.

KATHIE'S feelings for the first few days reminded her of her early visit to New York. There were so many strange sights and strange faces, ladies talking to her upon the one hand and gentlemen upon the other. She understood quickly how General Mackenzie was loved and honored. No wonder Ada had felt so proud of his notice that first evening at the opera. How had she been so fearless ?

She did not know that it was her own simple, truthful heart, so much sweeter and more attractive than all the world-polish that one can put on. For, although there may be much gilding and furbishing up and dazzling show that loudly demand the attention of passers by, the quieter grace and loveliness are not altogether forgotten. When the whole mass of mineral is crushed and fused, and the baser metals find their kindred attractions, a little quicksilver, you know, takes hold of the gold that has lain quietly amid all the smoke and bubbling, patiently biding its time.

There was so much going and so much sight-seeing that Kathie declared her brain was like a rubbish room, and that it would take weeks to get it into order. There were the country's palaces and halls, which, lacking the storied beauty of London and Paris, had still some brave and touching associations of their own. To her inexperienced eyes they were still magnificent.

A dozen times a day she said, "If Rob were only here," especially when they were going through the Treasury Department. General Mackenzie was the most charming guide imaginable. He seemed to know the history of everything, even that of many curiosities in the Patent Office, which somehow interested Kathie wonderfully. But she liked best of all to linger in the rotunda of the capitol. The great dome so high above her, the panels with their pictures, always chained her with a peculiar charm. There was the "Landing of the Pilgrims," with beautiful Rose Standish listening with wondering girlishness to the hoary patriarch giving thanks for the safe

ending of their perilous journey. How odd it seemed
to think of now as only a few days' sail !

And there was the White House with its sturdy
President. But Kathie could n't help thinking of
the other one, called to lay down his life for his
country's sake just as the morn of peace had begun
to dawn. And all the place seemed sacred to her for
the many precious souls of heroes and martyrs who
had risen up in the hour of need and done their duty
nobly.

There was a gay holiday side to it as well. To be
sure, a great many of the members had gone to rejoin
their families, but the streets were still thronged.
The storm was succeeded by several bright, sunshiny
days and a milder atmosphere. General Mackenzie
drove to all the points of interest outside of Washington, and described the appearance of it when it
was a grand camping-ground bristling with tents
and hospitals.

Mr. Winterdyne did not forget Kathie, but looked
in upon her several times, once bringing her some
exquisite hot-house flowers. Then she went out to a
number of grand dinners with Aunt Ruth and the
General, and altogether it was quite a gala time.

4

"Now you must see it in summer," General Mackenzie said. "Some time we will make another pilgrimage."

The visit seemed both long and short to Kathie. The time had passed rapidly and every sense had been crowded to repletion, and yet it was only a night or two ago that Mr. Winterdyne had handed her out of the dimly lighted cars to her uncle's cordial welcome. Now she was being handed in again.

The homeward journey was much more pleasant. No snowy shroud draped towns and villages and rivers. The crisp, keen air was wonderfully clear, and every distant tree or hill was outlined against the blue sky as if painted there.

They spent the night in Philadelphia, to Kathie's great delight, and took the following morning to ramble round, not arriving at Mr. Meredith's until dusk of the next day.

Jessie welcomed them both with smiles and kisses. "We thought you were never coming," she said. "We had quite a little feast yesterday in honor of you, but to-day it inclines to fragments."

"And I have been altogether superseded," declared Mr. Meredith. "The stars and bars and titles have won your heart, Kathie."

"No, it is n't that"; with an ingenuous blush. "And we talked of you while in Washington, and all the old times; and O, I met a friend of yours when I went on, a Mr. Miller, who was present at your marriage."

"Yes, he was here a few evenings since and told us. Kathie, you are quite a heroine."

"I don't know what for," she said, simply.

Mr. Meredith could have answered easily, but he did not wish to disturb the soft bloom of the peach before its midsummer ripening. It was her sweet unconsciousness of self, the bright, ready grace in ministering, that gave a beauty to the trifles of her daily life, and the spiritual correspondence back of it all.

"And you have had a nice time?"

"It has been more than nice," returned Kathie; "delightful, and just crowded full of enjoyment."

"Let them come up stairs and take off their wrappings," said matronly Jessie. "And Edward, if you will just call to Bridget, so that she can have things ready."

Mr. Meredith made a most ridiculous face, as if to ask Kathie's sympathy.

Jessie ran lightly up the stairs. The front room was a guest-chamber *par excellence*, and the folding-doors between this and her own room were thrown open. They looked so neat and pretty, with carpets of a soft rose-color and drab, and all the toilet mats embroidered with the same shades. The white curtains at the windows were plain muslin, with a bit of rose-color in the hems, while the ground-glass vases and scent-bottles were in purest white as well.

"Why, it looks like a fairy palace," declared Kathie. "And O, here are some flowers!"

"You would n't believe what a pretty conservatory I have down in the back parlor. I could not give up every nook to furniture. And here is my sewing-room."

A little nest off of Jessie's apartment, just as cosey as it could be, with a pretty willow workstand and a sewing-machine. There were some brackets and pictures against the walls, the latter Jessie's handiwork.

Aunt Ruth and Kathie had to inspect and admire everything. And here was another tiny vase of flowers.

"I don't want to fall into the mistake of putting every pretty article in my parlor for chance visitors to inspect. I desire little bits of beauty for myself; and as I sit and sew here, and listen to birdie singing or see a stray flower blossom, I feel as if life was an every-day glory, and not detached fragments of pleasure that you have hard work to piece together, and are in a continual fever lest the joinings will show."

"You are taking it up in the right way," said Aunt Ruth, with her sweet smile. "If we could all come to understand that the interior part of life, holding home and love, was so much more satisfying than outside show."

"Are you never coming down ? The General and I are half starved to death. We shall have to reorganize the regiment and appoint a new quartermaster."

They all marched down to the front basement, which served as dining-room. And even here Jessie's cunning hand was plainly visible. Bridget was quiet and tidy, and though her serving might not have had the grace of a French waiter, it was more lady-like than one might expect from a coarse-handed emigrant who had run wild and lived in the fields.

The journey and its wonders had to be told over, and Kathie's thorough delight made it very enter-

taining.   They sat a long while over their dessert, tor
there seemed no hurry, as is often the case.

" I have at last persuaded Bridget to eat her dinner
as soon as she brings on the dessert.   Sometimes she
even. goes so far as to wash up the dishes when we
have company, and now she thinks it so much nicer
than dawdling and hanging about," Jessie said to
Aunt Ruth.

" Have you had much trouble ? "

Jessie laughed.   " Bridget gave me notice at the
end of the first fortnight.   She had never lived in a
house where there was n't a chambermaid, and she
could n't do so much work ; but I believe she thinks
now that there is very little to do."

"Jessie will soon be qualified to write ' What I
know about Housekeeping,' " said Mr. Meredith,
laughingly.

" It will be very much needed," returned Aunt
Ruth.

The gentlemen stayed down to smoke a little
while, and Jessie took her guests back to the parlor.
Kathie was tired and sleepy, and laid her head in
Aunt Ruth's lap while the two ladies talked. Indeed, she was really glad to go to bed.

They spent most of the next day resting up. Mr.
Meredith came home early and took them to the
Park for a drive, and then went out with the Gen-
eral in the evening.

" I wish you would tell me about Ada," Kathie
said. " I should like to go and call upon her if — "

" If what ? " Jessie asked, curiously.

" If she would like it."

" I think she would feel a good deal hurt if you
did not. I am very sorry to see Ada take her reverse of fortune in so sore and hard a manner."

" But it must be a very sad thing."

" It is, indeed. It would be exceedingly trying to
me, and I am not so dependent upon outside surroundings. But Ada refuses utterly to be comforted.
She will not even accept the pleasures she might
have. She does not exert herself to make home
happy, and persuades herself that she is cut off from
everything beyond."

" But what does she do ? " asked Kathie.

" She reads a little, practises her music some, and
spends a good deal of her time in crying. You see,
nothing really interests her. She had expected to
devote her whole winter to dressing and society. It

is a great pity that she went to Saratoga last summer."

"Her friends have n't all given her up! That
would be too cruel."

"I dare say there are many who would still be
cordial, but she is very proud. I am not sure, Kathie, that learning to take is not just as necessary a
lesson in this world as learning to give. To accept
the pleasures friends are willing to put in our way,
even if we cannot return in kind."

"Yes," Kathie said, thinking it over. "It makes
you feel so happy when a person accepts anything
cordially."

"She is pale and thin and nervous to the last degree. Edward begged her to come up here for a visit,
and took us both to a concert; but she would not
stay, and, if she had, I should have been puzzled how
to entertain her. She has not the slightest resource,
and will not make any effort. Mrs. Meredith has so
much upon her hands that she cannot be looking
after Ada as if she were a little child. What a pity
to bring up a girl so entirely helpless!"

"Don't you suppose that Mr. Meredith will be rich
again some day?" Kathie asked.

"It will be years before they can go back again to the old style. Ada will be a faded invalid, good for nothing at all, unless she rallies soon. O Kathie, I am thankful every day for the full, fresh, country life I have had, and I do believe I enjoy all manner of refined pleasures with as great a zest as any one. Why, I went to a magnificent party on Christmas eve, — a grand Fifth Avenue affair, — and felt wonderfully at home, even if I had not been polished by Saratoga."

Kathie laughed gayly at that.

"The Merediths were invited as well, but Mrs. Meredith said they could not return anything of the kind, so they would not go. It was a very dear friend of Edward's, and he would not hear of our declining."

"But you liked it."

"Yes, a good deal, as one likes a curious entertainment. There was a great crowd, and every now and then some lovely train was stepped on and half ruined. There were flowers and pictures and an elegant supper, with one of the finest bands in the city for music. The ladies talked languidly, danced languidly, walked about as if they were half tired to death.

With all the beauty there was nothing fresh and stir-
ring that took hold of your heart and made you feel
as if you had had a good time. I was glad to get out
without damaging my beautiful dress that Edward
made me spend over two hundred dollars upon."

" Oh !" exclaimed Kathie, with a long breath.

"And that was absolutely nothing in the way of
cost. I really don't think it paid, except that I have
the dress. But last week we were invited to the
same house to a small dinner. There were eleven
guests, very charming, educated people. One lady
sang in the most exquisite manner, and another read.
I had for cavalier a gentleman fresh from China, who
entertained me delightfully, and I felt afterward as
if I had actually been somewhere."

Kathie's eyes kindled at this.

" So I have resolved in my life to have all the real
enjoyment that I can. The shams and make-believes
I shall let go."

" But I thought they used to be very happy at
Mrs. Meredith's."

" So they did. Their pleasures were very expensive, though, and now all plainer ones look common.
But if you would like to go, perhaps you had better

get ready, and I will take you. Afterward we can ramble around and look at some pictures."

Aunt Ruth did not mind being left at home, so Jessie and her guest started out, taking the horse-cars for some distance.

"The house is very pretty," said Kathie, ascending the high stone stoop. It did n't look as if they were very much reduced.

Inside Kathie recognized some of the old furniture and pictures, though she missed the elegance of the other drawing-room. Mrs. Meredith came in rather flurried, but handsome in attire.

"O Miss Kathie," she exclaimed, cordially, "how do you do? Why, this is quite a surprise. How glad Ada will be to see you. I will send up word to her immediately."

Katy was a long time in answering and a long time in doing her errand. And in the mean while Mrs. Meredith had gone through with some of her troubles. Florence had been sick all night with croup, the water-pipes had burst, they had been without a cook three days, and now had a miserable specimen, and the heater was so poor that you must either freeze up stairs or down stairs.

" I have never been accustomed to such inefficient
help," she said, loftily.   " First-class girls will not go
out for low wages, but I begin to think thirty dollars
a month would be cheaper for a good cook than twelve
for a poor one."

The door was opened slightly.

"Would Miss Alston please to walk up stairs?
Miss Ada had a headache, and could n't come down."

" Katy, how many times have I told you not to
open a door without knocking!" exclaimed Mrs.
Meredith, angrily.   " You never *can* beat anything
into their stupid brains."

Indignant Katy slammed the door in much the
same temper as her mistress.   Then she was summoned again, and commanded to show the visitor to
Miss Ada's room.

She only went as far as the nursery door.   " It is
the front room up stairs," she said, sullenly.

Kathie found it by herself, and tapped lightly.

" Come," answered a faint voice.

Kathie entered the room like a radiant little picture.   Her wine-colored suit, ermine muff and tippet,
and white felt hat trimmed with velvet and feather
the shade of her dress, were indescribably pretty and

becoming. Her loose light curls were gathered in a
knot at the back, with a few stray shorter ones around
her face. Her eyes were bright, her cheeks blooming
with a soft, peachy tint, and her skin pearly clear.
A very pretty girl indeed; but sweetest of all was
the earnest, tender, soulful expression. Yet Ada was
absolutely filled with envy, glad as she was to see
her.

The furniture and appointments of the room were
pretty enough, but it had a comfortless look. The
remnant of yesterday's fire was in the grate, while
the fender was filled with ashes and bits of torn
paper. The closet door was open, betraying the disorder within. Over the cushioned easy-chair was
thrown yesterday's dress and skirt, and at a little
distance stood her walking-boots. The top of the
bureau was in the utmost disorder. Collars, hand-
kerchiefs, ribbons, and a plate of breakfast fragments,
while from the side of the glass depended a net, a
braid of hair, and two straggling, fuzzy curls. How
different from the elegance in which Ada used to
pride herself!

The girls kissed in unaffected cordiality. Kathie's
generous heart was full of tenderest pity, the noble

kind that wounds not by pretentious showing, and anything so warm and bright seemed grateful to Ada just then.

" I am sorry to find you ill," Kathie said, gently.

" I have such wretched headaches ! And the house has been as cold as a barn all the morning. Katy has not found time to make up my fire yet, nor put my room in order. How dreadful it looks ! Can you find a chair ?" Ada was wrapped in a shawl and pillowed up in bed. She glanced around in dismay.

" Never mind," returned Kathie, pleasantly. " I am used to helping myself."

" How well you do look ! It is n't strictly aristocratic to have so much color, but it brightens up a chilly day like this. And I feel so — miserable ! O Kathie, you don't know what it is to be poor and to be deprived of all your comforts."

" Yes, I do," said Kathie, consolingly. " We were poor once, you know." " Much poorer than this," she felt like adding.

" But you had never been rich. You could not miss the ease and luxury as you would now."

" Mamma had," was her quiet response.

" I am sure I don't know what people do. I can-

not do anything. I went out to walk a little yesterday afternoon, but it tired me so. I have n't a bit
of strength. If this forlorn winter were only over!
You have been to Washington, have n't you?"

"Yes." Kathie was thinking it had been a very
charming winter.

"And your Aunt Ruth is married. I did not suppose she ever would be. General Mackenzie is really
your uncle. Did he introduce you to the elegant
people he knows? But I forgot — you are not in
society," with an air that only Ada could have used.

"We went everywhere — almost; and I saw gen-
erals and senators and beautiful ladies and the President, and such hosts of things."

"What a pity your Aunt Ruth is lame!" Ada said,
by way of bringing a skeleton to the feast.

"It is n't much. It scarcely shows now. And she
has grown so — lovely." It came out involuntarily,
and Kathie colored warmly.

"Society does so much for one," returned Ada,
with womanly assumption. "And it was so hard
for me to give it up just when I had begun. I had
such lovely times last summer. O dear!" Ada
wiped away a few tears.

"I can never tell you how sorry I was!" and Kathie gathered Ada in her arms, kissing the pale cheek.

"It was a terrible blow. In another year I should have been married, but now it has ruined everything. I feel sometimes as if I did n't care to live."

Kathie studied her in astonishment. "But you have your mother and father and — "

"As if troublesome children could do any one any good!" she exclaimed, pettishly. "Mamma has her hands full, and papa never has time for anything. Sometimes I do not see him for days together. Now and then some of the girls I used to like drop in, but they are always full of their own enjoyments. You see it would not have been so bad if I had actually been in society. I should have gone on having some nice invitations. But no one will ever hear about me now."

Kathie was sadly perplexed. How could she comfort Ada? "But there are a great many pleasant things," she began again, slowly. "You have your piano, and you used to be so fond of singing."

"I can't sing to myself, — at least there is no enjoyment in that. I did n't think I should ever want to

change places with you, Kathie Alston ; but I believe
I would be glad to now."

" It may all come back," exclaimed Kathie, brightly.

" I shall be old, and people won't like me then.   I
dare say I shall be an old maid."

Worrying about that when one was only sixteen
was rather ludicrous, Kathie thought.

Presently Jessie came up. Did not Kathie want to
go with her to call upon Dr. Markham ?

" I suppose it will be a good deal pleasanter than
staying here," said Ada.

" And if you will come and spend to-morrow with
us we shall be glad. If you cannot stay all night,
Uncle Edward shall bring you home in the evening."

After a deal of fidgeting and consideration Ada
partly consented ; if it was not too cold, and if her
head did not ache. So Kathie uttered a rather sad
good-by.

5

CHAPTER IV.

GLIMPSES OF GOLD AND GLIMPSES OF GRAY.

"I AM glad you thought of Dr. Markham," said Kathie, as they were once more in the street.

"Had you forgotten him?"

"O no. But I do not believe that I should have remembered him at this particular moment, and I am very happy to do it."

Her bright smile confessed the truth.

"Mrs. Meredith wanted me to stay to lunch, but I thought it best not. Is n't it odd that somehow I cannot feel as if she were my sister by law even, while I like Mr. Meredith so much. O, I wish they were happy for his sake, for all their sakes."

Kathie was silent, communing within herself What was lacking? An earnest purpose, something to do for one another, outside of their own purely personal lives. Mamma had been right in that old time, when she had taught her to study the comfort of Rob and Freddy a little. She saw now, with the larger eyes of girlhood's soul, that it had its beginning in a tiny bud way back there. All these kindly deeds for one another were an outgrowth towards the end, a process that was to nourish and bring forth good fruit, a vital, heartsome interest, a desire for the good of others, and not any mere selfish living for one's own gratification. " O," she said, thinking aloud in her earnestness, " if Ada only *could* see ! "

" Yes, she might do so much. And the worst is, that no one can tell just where this will end."

They soon arrived at Dr. Markham's. Mrs. Markham was delighted, and welcomed them warmly. "You must stay to lunch," she declared. " I will not hear a word. Only this very morning the Doctor was talking about Kathie. Why, child, how you have grown, — only you are Kathie still, and always will be. It is in the soul. And now tell me about Aunt Ruth and everybody."

They were still in the midst of an animated talk when the Doctor entered. His hair and beard were a trifle more grizzled, and the furrow in his brow a little deeper, but it was the same shrewd, kindly face.

" So you did n't forget your duty to your elders, —

is n't that catechism ?   I began to wonder if your
head had not been turned in Washington among all
the great men and grand dames.   Are you almost
ready to run away from us old fogies and set up an
independent line of behavior ? "

" I should run back the fastest," she said, archly.

He laughed. " I like that. We old people do
know something. We are not quite in our dotage,
although you try pretty hard to crowd us out. Have
you taken good care of Aunt Ruth and your famous
uncle ? Why did she not come with you ? or is she
afraid to face me after all her goings on ? Fine do-
ings, indeed ! Why, the city belles have been setting their caps for General Mackenzie years and
years."

Somehow, Kathie did feel just a little bit proud.

" Why, you are as rosy as a June day," he went
on. " Don't you know that such plumpness and
glowing tints are very old-fashioned ? You will
have to commence a course of ' German ' and late
dinners to reduce you. Have you seen Miss Ada ? "

" Yes ; we were there this morning."

" There is the style for you. Was n't she in bed
with a novel ? "

Kathie blushed.

"The same little telltale face," he continued, teasingly. "Why, I am afraid you will never make a society woman, any more than Mrs. Meredith here. And then we may look to see you go off and marry some poor fellow who can't stir hand or foot, as she did. What are we doctors going to do, I would like to know, if you persist in being so miserably healthy, and nursing all the sick folks well before we have run up half a bill?"

"It is very unfortunate," returned Kathie, with a bit of roguery in her eyes.

He took her arm to lead her in to lunch, and groaned over the fact of her being so tall. "There are enough young women in the world already," he said.

They had a gay time over their lunch. Then she must needs run up stairs and take a peep at the rooms where she and Aunt Ruth had spent one winter. Ah, how strange it seemed, how sweet and sad the days had been, how they had hoped and feared, and at last believed! and when we can do that the glory of heaven is all about us, the kingdom of heaven begun.

"I do not desire to be uncourteous, Mrs. Meredith," the Doctor exclaimed, as Jessie spoke of going, "but I have a lovely conspiracy formed in my own mind. I shall leave my little black 'Tiger' home to dust my books and polish my boots this afternoon, and take Miss Kathie. I will bring her back safe at dusk. Not a word now from either of you. I am very bad-tempered when any one crosses me, as Mrs. Markham can testify."

It seemed to Kathie that she had the merriest drive imaginable. He bundled her up in the lap blankets when he went in to see a patient, and she held the reins to perfection. Last of all, they took a turn around the park as the street lamps were being lighted, and then he had to stop and congratulate "Mrs. General."

Ada came the next day. Of course she was dressed beautifully, for there were stores of rich clothes that would be a harvest to fall back upon. But she paraded her nerves and her sorrows obtrusively, and Kathie had to summon her utmost good-nature to extract any honey from the visit, or even to bestow any.

General Mackenzie's most urgent business being concluded, they decided to return to Cedarwood a once, so Kathie could begin school the following week. Kathie felt very sorry, although she knew it was right. She had grown quite enchanted with this delightful, wandering life.

The home welcomes were very sweet, however. There were a few Christmas gifts, showing that they had not forgotten her, and so she dropped into the old niche.

It was very hard to stay in it contentedly. After all, it *would* be nice to be a grown lady, with no lessons and no particular hours claiming you, but just long, bright, happy years of freedom. Ah, was Ada happy?

Aunt Ruth's visit at Cedarwood could not last very long, for the General declared that he still had marching orders.

"I think in a year or two I shall leave the army," he said; "for there are younger men growing up to take my place, and I should like to enjoy a little home comfort before I die."

Kathie wrote a glowing account of the whole tour to Rob, who thought it must have been just about perfect. "But my turn will come some day," he replied. "I am getting to have a little more sense and patience than in the old times, and can wait with a better grace."

Another half-sweet, half-sad event had happened to Rob, and that was the visit of Mrs. Ludlow. Perhaps all the boys had learned a good lesson last term, for, though there was still a good deal of fun, it found a more harmless channel, and Dr. Goldthwaite began to feal really proud of his " first form " once more.

" I have been thinking," Rob wrote, " that, if mother was willing, I would like to have Mrs. Ludlow invited to Cedarwood next summer. She seems so down-hearted and lonely that it makes a fellow want to do something for her, and with us all she might be cheered up a bit."

" I am glad to see Rob willing to take upon himself a little of the finer part of duty, — courtesy," his uncle said. " I wanted to ask Mrs. Ludlow here last summer, but we were so nomadic that it was not possible."

Kathie did not forget old friends among all the new excitements. She and Emma Lauriston were growing into higher accord. Both gave and both took. Little flashes of knowledge came over them now and then, — self-knowledge and knowledge of each other. Emma had slowly studied out the great mystery, — was studying, I should say, for we all go on learning until the morning when the beautiful angel-warder of the other country opens wide the gates for us, and the earthly lore is transfused into the more glorious quickening and satisfaction of God's living presence.

Uncle Robert arranged some pleasant evenings for them, — little musical reunions. Several of the girls were very pretty singers, and Mr. Lawrence gave them an hour of regular practice. After that they amused themselves, and the fame of their amateur concerts went abroad until one and another begged to be present. They met at each other's houses, and broke up punctually at ten o'clock. Several young gentlemen joined the society, while Mr. Langdon and Uncle Robert gave it a kind of fatherly supervision.

Neither was Sarah Strong neglected. Perhaps, of all her pets and *protégés*, Kathie felt that she was likely to bring forth the most abundant fruit. The soil had appeared very unpromising at first, but the little leaven of a kindly word had roused the whole body into action. Mr. Strong kept declaring that he did not see the sense of it, that Sarah knew enough

for anybody; yet he was secretly proud of her ambi-
tion and her attainments. And when one Sunday,
in the absence of the regular musician, Sarah played
twice on the melodeon without a single mistake, his
fatherly heart was touched.

"And now I am going to have a melodeon of my
very own," Sarah wrote, delightedly. "It is n't a
piano, but it is next best, and we shall have nice
times singing with it on Sunday evenings. It is just
like a happy dream to me. Father wants me to ask
you what kind of a one is best, and what a good one
will cost. He thinks your uncle knows more than
any one else about everything."

"I did not suppose that I should ever have a **hand**
in the advancement of your young damsel," said Sue
Coleman, when the subject had been broached to Mr.
Lawrence at one of the musical evenings, "but I
know of something that may just fit in here. The
Cheltenhams have been buying a beautiful new Es-
tey organ, and want to sell their melodeon. It was
bought in cheap times, cost a hundred dollars, and
has two stops, beside being rich and sweet in tone.
It has not been injured any, and can be purchased for
seventy dollars."

"It is an excellent one," remarked Mr. Lawrence, "and will give good satisfaction. Your friend cannot do better."

Mr. Strong and Sarah came down one Saturday. He had "heard that you could get a pretty fair melodeon for fifty dollars, and Sarah would be wanting a new gown by and by, and ribbons and things — "

"O, I will go without them all!" Sarah exclaimed, in a tremor of excitement. "Why, it is almost as large as the one in church, and it is lovely. I would rather earn the twenty dollars some way."

"I don't know what has come over the girl," said Mr. Strong, "but she always does manage to have her own way. She is a good girl, though, and her larnin' has n't spoiled her a bit."

"I cannot make him say every word just right," Sarah whispered, blushingly; "but he has given up a good many of the old-fashioned habits. It is so nice to feel that you are a little like cultivated people."

So Sarah succeeded in getting her melodeon after much patient talking.

"She was so good and sweet about it," Kathie said, afterward. "Her whole heart was in it, yet she did not tease, and was not cross. And how wonderfully she has improved! Mamma, I think her quite a good-looking girl."

"That is exactly it, Kathie, — good-looking; and often that is really better than beauty."

One morning Lou Rossiter surprised them with an astounding piece of news. "Belle Hadden is married," she announced, "and there is quite a romance about it. She met a French count in Baltimore, who pretended to be very rich, and the affair culminated in a grand wedding."

"And he turned out to be somebody's valet," interpolated Sue.

"Not quite so bad as that; but he was poor, and dreadfully in debt, and very angry that ma'm'selle had no dowry. So they quarrelled, and Belle went back to her mother."

"What a sad thing!" was Emma's comment.

"Moral: Beware of French counts," added some one else.

Kathie missed Aunt Ruth everywhere, and, most of all, in the garden when spring came. It did not seem half as delightful to her to work alone, for Mrs. Alston could not be out a great deal with her daughter; and Kathie, being much engrossed with her studies, turned the matter over to Mr. Morrison.

Ethel's father had gone West to claim his tract of government land and settle upon it. He was very well and prospering nicely.

Several of the larger girls in school would graduate this year, and leave. That was another sad thing for Kathie.

"There are so many changes all the time," she said, disconsolately, to Uncle Robert. "I believe I would like to be a little child again, or a woman."

"You cannot be the child, but you are going rapidly to the other bound. And I shall be very sorry to lose my bright little fairy."

"It is so strange, — all the life, and the going on, and the being something to-day that you were not yesterday. It puzzles me. I feel at times as if I hardly dared to take a step."

"God gives us grace and strength, my darling, if we ask of him. And if we keep in the shadow of his great love, we cannot go very far astray."

There was a certain thoughtful intentness in Kathie's eyes that was still more question than satisfaction.

" Is the puzzle there yet, little one ? " asked Uncle
Robert, kindly.

" It is about the fruit, Uncle Robert.   When I am
very happy and in the midst of pleasure I am afraid
I do not think of it, and when the enjoyment is over
the work looks a little bit — hard.   But I don't
want to live a barren, useless life, or a purely selfish one."

" My dear, it is not the fruit season yet with you,
but rather spring and the planting-time.   And in the
Lord's gardening there is much for delight and orna-
ment and refreshment.   If we looked at the duties
only, I am afraid we should become cold and rigid ;
so he wills that we shall have the pleasures as well,
only the idleness must not unfit us for work."

Kathie tried with a very earnest heart.   There
were many discouragements with herself, to be sure.
but it is step by step in this life, and not a wide
going from one phase to another.

The nearer Rob came to the end of the term the
more glowing his accounts were.   " I have worked
like a Trojan," he wrote to his uncle, " but I have
achieved something by it.   I am going in strong for
one of the prizes, and I have the Latin oration.   I

want you and mother to come, for I think you may
justly be a little proud of me now."

" And we must surely go," said Uncle Robert.

It so happened that Mrs. Wilder's school closed at
the same time this year.

" It is too bad," Kathie declared, " but I would a
great deal rather have you go to Clifton Hall, though
ours will be very much nicer than last year. But
Rob must not be disappointed."

They did have a very appreciative and quite a
large audience. The graduating class acquitted
themselves finely, and reflected much credit upon
Mrs. Wilder. There were bouquets and compliments,
and satisfaction was expressed in every form. Quite
a number of the girls were invited to Mrs. Coleman's
afterward. Kathie had been delegated to ask Mr.
Langdon.

" It is not a real party," Sue said, " but a little
supper and a little talk."

So Mr. Langdon and Kathie called for Emma, who
looked very neat and simple in her white dress.

" You take your honors very meekly, Miss Lauriston," Mr. Langdon said. " I thought you one of the
stars of the occasion."

"Because I happened to have a special gift. I did not study any harder than the other girls, and in some branches I really had superiors."

"And now are you going to neglect your talents, after the fashion of young ladies?"

Emma colored. "It is rather hard to find out what to do in this world," she said, slowly. "The women who are rich can indulge their tastes, and those who are very poor take the first thing that offers, since they must work. But it is quite difficult for those between."

"Then you don't feel inclined to use Agur's prayer?" and he smiled a little.

"I think I would like to have the riches *now*. I want to study art. Even if I could go to the School of Design —"

"Well, why don't you? It seems to me that it would be an excellent step, and one in the right direction."

There had been a great struggle in Emma's mind about this matter. She hesitated a little now.

"Have you not sufficient courage?"

"It is not that." Her voice was quite low, and she felt somehow as if she wanted to get hold of Kathie for a touch of the strength she needed.

"What then?" Mr. Langdon seemed to feel very curious, or a great deal interested.

"I would like it very much, but I think I ought not go away and leave grandmother. They were so good to us when we were first left orphans; and grandfather has done all that he could for Fred. I feel as if I ought to stay with them until — until my money comes to me, for they could not help both of us."

"Yes, you are right," he answered, quietly. "But you must not give up entirely. If I were an artist, I might offer you some instruction, but I have only a great love for it, and a little cultivation. Still, I should like to drop in now and then and note your progress."

"You are very kind," Emma returned, with a shy tremulousness.

"I don't know as it was quite proper," she said to Kathie, as they were taking off their hats in Sue's room. "I have caught that exceeding honesty from you, Kathie Alston; and it seems so much easier now to tell a straight-out truth than to make elegant and evasive excuses. But it does seem to me that Fred ought to have what little there is. I wish

6

Grandmother Kellar had been more generous all
along, and not been anxious for me to have so much
when I am twenty-one."

Sue's little party was quite a success. The young
ladies were complimented over again, there was music and singing, two or three quadrilles, and a very
social supper. Here and there, in small knots, the
girls discussed what they were going to do during
the summer. And Kathie wondered a little what
her pleasures would be.

Mr. Langdon watched them with a peculiar interest. How many of them would mar their bright
young lives!

CHAPTER V.

WHICH, — HERSELF, OR HER NEIGHBOR ?

" HURRAH !" exclaimed Rob. " That is all done
with, and it was the grandest sort of a go ! Everything just right, and a prize, and a good deal of common sense hammered into my brain along with the
uncommon. Old Goldy did the handsome thing by
me, I tell you ; but I *have* tried to be good and persevering this year, and I begin to think you *can* do
a good deal when you try."

Kathie kissed him again and again. What a great,
bright-looking fellow he was ! His hard work had
not told much upon him.

It was easy to see that Mrs. Alston was delighted.
Dr. Goldthwaite's account of him was really flatter-
ing.

" He has been among the best boys in school this
year," he said. " I never saw a boy more resolute
and earnest. You need not be afraid to trust him
anywhere."

This was most encouraging. To be sure, all the
larger and more subtile temptations of life were yet
to come ; but they had a hope that, having once
begun, he would fight manfully to the end.

The boys were all home, and for a week quiet Silver Lake echoed with a bedlam of noises. It seemed
as if the whole crowd were wild. Mrs. Alston looked
on in astonishment. Uncle Robert laughed.

" It is only the reaction," he exclaimed.

" But they are so large now, — almost young men."

" I am glad the boyish element has not been quite
eradicated. After nine or ten months of study they
need a very thorough relaxation."

Indeed, Kathie could get nothing out of them.
They scorned croquet and girls with superb dignity.

Rob had earned his gun over again. At least, he
had kept his promise for a year, and meant to keep
it, he declared, solemnly.

And then came the old question : " What are we
going to do ? "

" I have an invitation for Rob," said his uncle.
" Several days ago I received a letter from General
Mackenzie, who has gone out to look after the Indian
treaties. Bruce is to spend some weeks with his

father, as his year's hard work rather tells upon him; and the General proposes that Rob shall accompany him."

"That is altogether magnificent! Three cheers!"

"But they cannot go alone!" suggested Mrs. Alston, in dismay.

Uncle Robert laughed.

"O mother, you think we shall always be, like the babes in the wood, getting lost."

"But such a long journey!"

"Not a difficult one, however."

"O, we shall do well enough. It will be just royal. To think of going out to the forts and seeing the Indians —"

"In all their native glory," interrupted Kathie, laughingly.

"The noble red men of dime novels! I don't believe quite so firmly in those romances. Why can't you go too, Uncle Robert?"

"What would Kathie do?"

"O, make a family party."

"I believe we have not been invited," Uncle Robert replied, mirthfully. "Aunt Ruth might not be able to enlarge her housekeeping borders on so short a notice."

Kathie's eyes were glistening. How delightful it would be to go! and she almost wished she was a boy.

"It is settled then, I suppose," said Rob. "When are we to go, and what do we need?"

"Bruce will be ready about the middle of July, and meet us in New York. Kathie and I will go down to see you off."

"I hope you will have something nice," Rob said, afterward, to Kathie. "But this is the most splendid thing I could have imagined. I *did* feel a little jealous when you went to Washington and had such a good time, but this makes it about even."

"I am glad for your sake"; and so she was. No doubt there would be pleasures for her.

One came before very long. Mrs. Coleman and quite a party were going to the White Mountains. She came over herself to see if Mrs. Alston and Mr. Conover would join them, and she proposed to invite Emma Lauriston as well.

"I don't know," Kathie said, dubiously. "It would be delightful, and I would like to go; and if Mr. Meredith and Jessie would —"

Uncle Robert smiled over the perplexity.

" Suppose we leave it until we have been to New York, then."

She went to see how Emma was likely to decide.

" It was very kind indeed in both Sue and Mrs. Coleman to think of me. I would like to go, above all things — almost — only — "

Emma paused there and colored.

" It *is* a disappointment, but I am going to give it up," she began again, bravely. " I really do not think that I ought to afford it. Then Fred is coming home in a few days. I know by what he says that he has studied himself almost to death. He just wants a nice quiet time here in the old house with grand-mother and me, so when I read that it decided me at once. Maybe I can go some other time."

Emma's eyes were lustrous with tears that she was trying her best to keep back.

" Yes," Kathie returned, quietly. " I am not sure that we shall go, either."

" But you are not going to stay on my account," exclaimed Emma, with quick apprehension.

" No. Don't feel troubled about that. We are going to New York for a few days, and it will not be positively settled until we come back."

Rob had a great time packing up, and, as usual, his mother had to take it in hand. The boys bewailed him loud and deep, and Freddy thought it a great shame that he could not go out and see the Indians and hunt buffaloes. And it was cruel that he could not even go to New York.

Mrs. Alston was rather thankful when the bustle was at an end. Her big boy seemed to make a great stir everywhere. He was so full of vigorous life and fun, and had such a breezy way that there could be no quiet where he was. And yet she could hardly give a cordial assent to this long absence.

Mr. Meredith was very much surprised at his growth and improvement. Bruce met them on the same day, and Uncle Robert secured their tickets and sketched a little plan for the journey. They could take care of themselves, of course, almost young men as they were, for Bruce's stronger consideration would temper Rob's headlong impetuosity.

"I am sorry not to be able to come to Cedarwood," Bruce said, in a little aside to Kathie. "I was so in hopes that father could spend the summer there. Mind, I shall write to you very often, and you must answer."

Kathie promised.

"I shall not believe that I really have a mother until they are settled somewhere, keeping house in true orthodox style. And it is oddest of all to think that we are actually cousins."

Kathie blushed warmly at that, and could not decide whether she felt like a cousin or not.

"Now we will have a little visiting by ourselves," Jessie said, when they were finally disposed of in a railroad car. "Aunt Ruth will have her hands full with those two great boys, even if she only sews on buttons and finds their lost traps. But they will have a grand good time. And now tell me about everybody."

Kathie mentioned among other things the invitation. "If you could go, I should like to," she said.

"That would not be possible. I may go home for a fortnight or so, but Edward will not be able to leave the business. George is to be gone about a month."

"How is Ada? There have been so many things on my mind that they have rendered me neglectful."

"Poor Ada! Even Dr. Markham is beginning to feel alarmed about her."

"She is not ill?"

"The worst kind of illness. She takes no interest in anything or anybody. She has no appetite, no strength, is despondent and listless. Her father proposed taking her with him, but she did not want to go. They are to board at a quiet little sea-side place, but she does not care for that, either. She has wasted away to a shadow. I wish something could be done to rouse her."

"Does Dr. Markham think she has any settled disease?"

"He is afraid of her going into consumption. He took her out to drive in the spring, but after two or three excursions she declared that she would never go again with such a cross old bear. He rails so at fashionable life and follies, you know, and all the indolence and nervousness that follow. Still, he does take a fatherly interest in the poor child. Is n't it odd? — here he comes now."

"Talk of angels," said Kathie, laughingly.

Jessie opened the hall door herself.

"No, I am not an angel, Miss Kathie," he declared, "but much nearer a porcupine. Perhaps it was the rustling of my quills you heard."

"Rob would quote Byron," said Jessie, mirthfully.
"'The car rattling o'er the stony street.'"

"But there is no one to dance," responded the Doctor. "I heard that you had just sent your young
Arabs to the Rocky Mountains."

"Not quite so far as that," said Kathie.

"We were speaking of Ada," Jessie began, presently. "When are they going away?"

"Goodness knows! That child has more whims
than forty old women! I wish I could be her mother for a few months. Miss Kathie, suppose you drive
down there with me? The sight of such a blooming
face ought to do any one good."

Kathie glanced at Jessie.

"We have just begun *our* visit," the latter answered. "Will not to-morrow do?"

"You can begin over again," he said brusquely.
"Beginnings are about the pleasantest events there
are in life. Maybe Ada will not want her for more
than ten minutes."

So Kathie went for her hat, and gave Jessie an
unobserved kiss.

It was a warm afternoon, and Kathie missed the
shady trees and fragrant country air. Mr. Meredith's

house was in a pleasant row, to be sure, and here were other quiet squares, but everything looked parched and dusty in this midsummer heat.

"Kathie," the Doctor exclaimed, abruptly, "you are a sort of missionary, are you not?"

"A missionary!" Kathie's face was scarlet.

"Yes. Don't you suppose there are any this side of China?" and he gave her an odd glance out of his shrewd eyes.

"Why — of course."

"But you have n't taken your degree yet, — is that it?"

Kathie's eyes drooped thoughtfully.

"There is not the slightest need of Ada's dying. It will be a sort of slow, foolish suicide, and yet I don't know but she is bent upon it. And she surely will unless she is roused in time."

"But what could I do?" asked Kathie, perplexed.

"I cannot tell exactly what; only seeing you so bright and fresh brought the thing into my mind. What did you do to keep your Aunt Ruth alive?"

"It is so different, though."

"Yes. She did not need to be taught anything. But Ada is like a baby, — worse even in her ignorance. What is her education good for, her accomplishments ? Why, she does n't understand the commonest principle of life, the commonest duty. She ought to be a comfort to both her parents ; instead, she is only an anxiety."

"Dr. Markham," Kathie said, coming bravely to confession, "I do not think that Ada and I are — true friends. There is always some gulf between us, and we cannot seem to get over it."

"Who, — you, or she ? " and a kind of grim smile curved his lip.

" Both, perhaps."

"Don't you suppose the great Master saw the gulf as well ? And yet he went on."

Kathie was revolving it in her mind.

" What I mean is," she said, in a slower and lower tone, "that we don't quite suit. She does n't like the things that I like, and I am afraid that I could not interest her in anything that was real earnest and true. If I could I would be very glad to."

"I guess Ada has taken the lead heretofore. You stood a little in awe of her because they were very grand and fashionable, and you took her fine ways rather meekly. It was only on the outside, though,

for I heard about your not singing there one Sunday
evening, and how you stood in the front, exposed to
all the fire, and never flinched."

Kathie's curls drooped lower over her crimson face.

" The world has changed with them, you see. Ada's
fine friends have dropped off, and she had none beside. Mrs. Meredith is learning a useful lesson as
well, but she is older and has more resources. Still,
she is much engrossed with her other children and
her household cares, and perhaps understands Ada
no better than you do. Are you going anywhere this
summer ? "

Kathie hesitated, almost guessing what must come
next. It would be so easy to plead a partial engagement, but she felt in her heart that they would not
be likely to go to the White Mountains, after all. It
looked mean to make it an excuse.

" I think we shall be very likely to stay at home."

" Going to the seaside will not do anything for
Ada. She may bathe a little, but she will not get
interested in any one, nor come out of the gray
shadow of self. Indeed, she rather shrinks from
the experiment. She said, a few days ago, she
thought she should like to go to Brookside if her

auntie went, and seeing you brought the thing into
my mind. Suppose, between you both, you should
try to entertain her for a month."

"If I could do her any good — "

"You can try. The world is full of poor, miserable wretches who must be saved somehow, and most
of them saved from themselves. And I do believe
that a good many of these things come back to one.
What is it, — bread upon the waters ? I dare say
you know more about it than I. Here we are."

They had been driving very slowly, taking the
shadiest streets. He paused before the door, and the
two boys rushed out with a shout of joy.

"O, it is Miss Kathie ! Why, you have n't been
here ever and ever !" declared Willie, jumping up the
step and holding a not over-clean face to be kissed.

"There, don't eat her up. She has come to see
Ada to-day. Give her a chance to step on the side-
walk."

"She always comes to see Ada," said George, rather
discontentedly. "Only you *did* use to tell us stories.
I have remembered all about the prince and the little
white fairy until now. O, can't you stay down in
the parlor ? Mamma and Florrie have gone out, and
we will have a real good time."

"Not to-day, little men," said the Doctor, shielding Kathie from the rapturous embraces. "We must see Ada instead. I would go out and play again, if I were you."

Dr. Markham led Kathie up stairs. Ada was sitting in a rocking-chair by the window.

"There, I have brought you some one as sweet and fresh as a June rose, or a whole garden of flowers. If you are not thankful, I will carry her off again!"

Ada rose languidly. She had grown taller during the last six months, but was now very thin and seemed scarcely able to support herself. Her face was small and deathly pale, with purplish circles under her eyes, and a wan, feverish look in them.

"Why, this is a surprise," she said, kissing Kathie with affection. "But I don't see how you came to stray in town when everybody else is straying out. You are not tired of green fields, surely?"

Kathie explained.

"Now," exclaimed the Doctor, looking at his watch, "I am going to leave you two girls for an hour or so, when I shall come back after Kathie, as I left Mrs. Jessie broken-hearted. So talk fast."

Kathie was really shocked with the change in Ada,

and the kind of wistful expression went to her heart at once. She did indeed look very delicate. Her fingers were slender enough for the most rigid requirements of fashion, and white enough, too, for that matter.

The room was quite tidy and pleasant. Instead of the careless girl they had a very efficient woman, who rather admired Miss Ada, but considered her "not long for this world."

"How glad I am to see you!" Ada said, with much interest. "And so Bruce Mackenzie has gone off to have a visit with his new mother. How odd it seems that the General's wife should be your Aunt Ruth! And you know you met him that night when you were at the opera with me. It is like a story-book, — is n't it ?"

"A good deal better," returned Kathie. "It is all real, and they are very happy."

Ada sighed. "Everything has changed terribly since then. I only went to two operas last winter."

"And I did n't go to any," said Kathie, cheerily.

"But you were in Washington. Where will your uncle take you this summer ?"

"Perhaps we shall not go anywhere."

7

"Tell me about the Brookside girls and boys. It is so seldom that any one comes in to talk to me."

Kathie described their graduating class and its success and Sue Coleman's little party. "They have planned a trip to the White Mountains," she added.

"I don't envy them. It seems such an undertaking to go climbing about; though if one were well it would make a difference. I don't even want to go to the seaside."

"Why?"

"I believe I begin to hate strange faces and all that. I would like to hide away where it was beautiful and quiet, and no one stared at me when I went to the table, and there was some one to talk with. I never feel well any more, you know, and I cannot stand the slightest exertion."

"But if you could — make a little — " Kathie said, hesitatingly.

"I can't. The least thing tires me to death. The only pleasure I should enjoy would be carriage riding. I suppose you have your ponies yet?"

"O yes, and ever so much enjoyment with them."

"You are a fortunate girl, Kathie Alston. I wish I had such health and spirits, — yes, all, for it seems to me you cannot have a bit of pleasure if you are poor."

" But a great many do," was the rather timid response. " And we were quite happy while we were poor."

Ada glanced at her as if she was studying something, and could hardly get at the central truth upon which the whole structure was reared.

" I don't understand it," shaking her head.

Kathie did not try to explain. She felt that it would be like planting seed before the ground was prepared. But she went on talking of matters that she fancied would not be uninteresting to Ada, and succeeded so well that Ada could hardly believe an hour and a half had elapsed since Dr. Markham left them.

" How long are you going to stay ? " asked Ada. " Do come to-morrow and take lunch with us. I do hate to have you go away."

Kathie promised.

" I would n't mind taking you to the Park afterward for a drive, if you will both promise to be very good."

Kathie accepted eagerly, and Ada did not dissent.

"I am not going to ask you what you think until
to-morrow night," said the Doctor. "You are a little
bunch of sunshine, and if you don't go about brightening the world, you will certainly miss your voca-
tion. So don't set up for a comet, with fancy stream-
ers and zigzag ways."

She laughed a little, and yet she was rather grave
during the brief drive. Uncle Robert and Jessie
were watching for her, and gave her a sweet, smiling
welcome. "Little runaway, we thought we should
have to set out on a search for you," he said.

"As if she could stay away from the Prince forever," Jessie made answer, smilingly.

CHAPTER VI.

SOWING ON STONY GROUND.

KATHIE was considering how she could manage to have a good talk with Uncle Robert, when he said, "It is a lovely moonlight evening. Would you not like to take a walk in the Park, or are you too tired?"

"O no, I should be delighted."

"I see that you are forgetting me rapidly," exclaimed Mr. Meredith, in a make-believe injured tone, which sounded so real that Kathie started.

"Quote to him 'Not that you love Cæsar less, but Rome more,'" appended Jessie, laughingly.

"I do not mean to forget anybody," she said, with slow gravity.

"My little friend, I think I know that"; and he gave her the old sweet smile. Then, bending his head a little lower, he whispered, "I see you have something on your mind that Uncle Robert only can settle; so go get the tangle smoothed out of it."

They walked quietly along a few squares, and then

turned into the broad entrance. The winding roads looked like streams of silver in this tender light, and the trees rustled softly to the monotone of the south-wind. How beautiful it was! How glorious the whole world was when God's love was seen in it and through it! The earth and all the fulness thereof was made for human souls, that they might gather the spiritual manna after the type of the old Israel-ites, never having any lack, and yet providing for the day only; for to-morrow it would be flooded again with waves of light and glory and love.

"How quiet you are!" Uncle Robert said, at length.

"Am I? I was thinking, and it puzzles me"; with a slow accent on the last words.

"I suppose the end is somewhere with which you can unravel it all."

"It is about Ada. Uncle Robert, would it be very foolish if I did not go to the White Mountains?"

"Why, no, child, if there is anything pleasanter for you."

"I don't know as it will be pleasanter for me or anybody. And I cannot tell whether I want to do it or not, even if you were all willing."

"I think I understand the state of mind, but what is the project?"

"First, I will tell you about my call this afternoon, and my talk with Dr. Markham," she said, repeating it in her simple, straightforward manner.

"So the vexed question is, whether you will invite Ada, and devote your summer to her, or choose something that you would enjoy really better."

"What would mamma think of it?"

"I believe she does n't care much about joining Mrs. Coleman's party, though she would for your sake."

"I think I shall not go, then, whatever else I may do," she made answer, quietly.

"And if you loved Ada very much this would be a great pleasure; but at present it is a kind of duty for her welfare."

"She does n't want to go to the seaside. She is very nervous, and the children fret her, and she cannot bear the thought of being among strangers. Dr. Markham says she needs quiet and a little pleasant diversion and excitement, — to be roused out of herself. I don't know as I could do any of it, but —"

"Dr. Markham is a true physician, — a healer of souls as well as bodies. We owe him something for his kind care of Aunt Ruth. And if you were willing to undertake it, — since the most troublesome part must fall upon you."

"You do not think that mamma would object?"

"I will answer for her. But, Kathie, suppose it is a trouble and perplexity, and brings forth no good result, — how shall you feel then?"

"I don't believe I am a bit sanguine, Uncle Robert. It does n't seem as if I could do anything much for Ada, for our thoughts and wishes and enjoyments are so different. Only there is the lovely place, the quiet house, the ponies, and no one very rich or grand to fret her. I would try to do my best."

"Perhaps it is worth an effort. It is the poor and needy we are to save, and those from the lanes and by-ways that we are to ask in to our feasts. There may be great poverty of soul and much straying into perverse and crooked paths without absolute pecuniary indigence. I sometimes think the rich people need to have missionaries sent among them as well as the poorer ones."

"Then I may do it, if it seems best? Ada may not want to come, to be sure."

"I would talk it over with Jessie to-morrow, and learn what she thinks."

They had rambled to the lake by this time, and paused to study the clear waters that seemed alive with stars shining in the quivering depths. They both felt the beauty, but they had no heart to talk about it then; and though Uncle Robert understood better than she how truly generous her proposal was, praise would have marred the sweet, noble charity of it.

By and by they turned and walked homeward. Jessie had spread out a cunning little quartette table with dainty China saucers and cream. After that Kathie played a game of backgammon with Mr. Meredith, and, as it was a rather tight squeeze, managed to beat him by a solitary one left on the board.

Jessie and Kathie had their talk the next morning.

" I cannot decide whether it is sheer perverseness in Ada, or not," Jessie said. " If I had proposed that she should go to Brookside, I dare say she would have thought the place insufferably dull, and declined. She is excessively 'notional,' and in very poor health, brought about by her own indolence and selfishness. If we all made self the central figure, what a world it would be ! "

This rather damped Kathie's ardor.

"Perhaps I don't feel quite as patient as I should, since Ada has refused nearly every effort of mine to make her life a little brighter."

"She may have come to a different mood," said Kathie.

"Well, it is very sweet and generous of you to be willing to give up so much time for her entertainment. And that is where your duty comes out sunbright."

A lovely smile broke over Jessie's face as she uttered this.

Kathie was thinking of the great Exemplar, "who pleased not himself." And life was not a mere matter of gathering the rose that grew directly in one's way.

So, when she was going over to Ada's, Jessie remarked, "I will commission you to say anything that you can for me, and I will abide by it."

Ada was very low-spirited at first. She had been crying half of the morning. It was a warm, rather sultry and depressing day, and she was in a state to suffer from everything while she kept thinking so steadily about herself.

"I don't believe I ever shall get well," she said, despondingly. "No one realizes how my health is failing. To be sure, there does n't seem much worth living for when you have to give up all the things that interest you. I sometimes think it would not be much harder to die."

Kathie started at that. Life seemed such a blessed and glorious thing to her.

"Is n't it cooler down stairs?" she asked, presently. "It seems so warm up here, next door to the sun."

"I seldom do go down before lunch-time. Mamma is out finishing up the shopping. I have heard about seaside until I am tired and sick of it."

"We might go down to the parlor and look over some of the old books. I suppose you do not study any nowadays? Have you given up the languages and everything?"

"O, what is the use of bothering one's brains! I shall never have occasion for them again. And I was getting along so beautifully in my Italian music; but if one is to be shut out of the world forever — "

"I don't believe any one is compelled to be," said Kathie, gently. "There are always some nice people — "

"You do not know much about it — here," Ada returned, with an air of dignified, world-weary experience. "Country places are different."

Kathie persuaded and entreated in her cunning fashion, which had in it so much sweetness that presently Ada was won into going down stairs. It was much cooler. The room was in very nice order, except that a glass of faded flowers stood on the centre-table.

"O dear," Ada exclaimed, fretfully, "papa brought them home for me. I dare say they never had a drop of fresh water yesterday. I asked Mary to bring them up to me, but she is just as likely to forget as to remember. And mamma knows how fond I am of flowers."

Why could she not have thought of it herself, if she valued the gift? Kathie colored with conscious and perhaps unkind criticism in her thoughts.

She rolled the *tête-à-tête* over by the window and arranged a pillow for Ada, chatting in a way that would have seemed very easy and unrestrained to a third person, but she did have to make a great effort to keep her voice so sunny and clear.

Mary tapped at the door directly.

" Miss Ada," she said, in a pleasant tone, " would
you not like to have your lunch brought up here ?
Your mamma has not come home yet, and the children may be a trouble — "

" That will be very pleasant, Mary. I am glad you
thought of it."

" How much better you look, Miss Ada ! " and
Mary smiled. " I wish you could have company
every day."

She arranged a small table in the back parlor, and
brought up a few delicacies. Ada had but little
appetite and merely tasted, and Kathie felt almost
ashamed of her hunger, — the result of perfect health
and good habits.

Afterward she read to Ada a long while. It
seemed as if she had at last hit upon something
satisfying. Mrs. Meredith dropped in and chatted
a few minutes, gratified to find her daughter in so
pleasant a mood.

They were quite ready to go out when Dr. Markham came.

" Kathie has stolen my art," he declared, in bluff
good-humor. " What has she done to you ? Why,
if I am not careful, I shall lose my patient and have

no one to drill me into good-mannered ways. You look as bright as a daisy."

"But I can't have Kathie always," Ada said, with a little longing in her tone. "I believe I do feel better. You see, I get so very lonesome, not being able to go out any."

"You must brighten up and find a young and handsome escort, not an old bear like me. Well, where are your traps? Doctors don't have much time to waste upon compliments."

"I will send Mary for them."

"Let me go," exclaimed Kathie. It appeared to her that Mary had been up and down stairs a thousand times at least during the day. On the way she stopped to kiss Florence and give her a tender little squeeze.

The ride was a success certainly. Ada even consented to go to dinner at Aunt Jessie's, though she was pretty tired when they reached the house.

"I think you can do it," Dr. Markham whispered to Kathie, with a shrewd smile.

It came out some way at the dinner-table, helped along a little by Uncle Robert's kindly tact, that Ada should come to Brookside with her aunt and uncle, and then spend a few weeks with Kathie, not going to the seaside at all.

"It would be much pleasanter," she said, "only I am afraid mamma will not agree to it." She had fallen into the habit of conjuring lions out of any little wayside shadow.

"I will see to that," replied her uncle.

He took her home later in the evening.

"Kathie, you must have bewitched her," he said, afterward. "I have not seen Ada so like herself in a long while. I wish the child could get a little common sense in her head before it is altogether too late. But it is a grand moral conversion for her to want to go to Brookside. Last summer she held herself immeasurably above it."

Kathie kept the Doctor's conspiracy to herself. He had only planned a little, set the wheels in motion, and the rest had come about itself. She sincerely hoped that it would all be for the best.

They returned home the next day.

"Dear, lovely Cedarwood," Kathie said, betwixt smiles and tears, "there is n't another place in all the wide world so beautiful and so dear!" And then, in her mind, she ran over the greater events since their coming. Not one lasting, heartfelt sorrow, but O, so many joys! Could she ever be thankful enough?

Sue was a good deal disappointed, much more than Kathie had thought possible.

"You are such a sort of comfortable little midget that you could help a body find out all the bright places, and you would be excellent for a rainy day. I have half a mind to kidnap you and take you off in spite of yourself."

Kathie laughed archly. Yet it was very pleasant to be needed and wanted.

Fred Lauriston had come home in her absence. He was taller than Rob, but O so thin and pale, and his eyes had a kind of feverish stare that was very uncomfortable.

"I am afraid he is really ill," Emma said, anxiously. "Grandfather was so shocked. But Fred insists that a little of the old-fashioned country life will make him all right again. I am so glad that you are not going away. He wondered if we might have Rob's boat."

"Yes, indeed, anything. And you must come over as often as you can. Ada Meredith is to be here, and she is an invalid too. We will have a regular hospital."

"Oh!" exclaimed Emma, in a tone of disappointment. "There are some people in the world that you cannot take to cordially, and Ada is one. Why did she want to come this particular summer?"

"She may never have another summer," Kathie said, slowly.

Emma shivered. "I cannot bear to think of any one's dying, and in summer most of all."

Every one seemed a little regretful when it was known who was to have the first claim upon Kathie. She visited industriously in the few days of grace remaining, taking up several of her old playmates, who somehow had strayed off during her last busy year.

Charlie Darrell came over one evening to say that Jessie and Mr. Meredith and Ada had arrived.

"She looks like a walking ghost," he exclaimed; "worse even than poor Fred."

Mrs. Alston had quietly acquiesced in Kathie's plans. In truth, she much preferred this to the fashionable rambling about with the Coleman party for so young a girl as Kathie. It was rather too soon to throw her into the temptations of the world, the vanities, jealousies, and petty detractions that narrow the soul and harden the heart and brain. Let her

8

keep pure and fresh, even if she were less wise and less mature.

The journey had fatigued Ada a good deal. For several days she kept to the bed or sofa. Every one, even to grandmother, vied in kindness. She was capricious and desponding. To-day she fancied that she had too much company ; to-morrow, that she was neglected.

" It will be so different when you are able to ride out," Kathie said, cheerily. "And I want you to come over and get fairly settled at Cedarwood before Mr. and Mrs. Meredith go back."

" I am sure we would do everything in our power for her," exclaimed grandmother. " Poor dear young thing ! What a pity ! I wonder if the people who have such sensitive nerves ever think that others have any at all ? "

They were not apt to, Kathie suspected. She had a fancy that Ada would feel more at home with her.

But when she was a little rested and began to go out there was a decided change. Dick Grayson came over to call upon her, and Charlie was quite a chivalrous escort, more from the natural kindness of his heart than any real admiration.

"For Kathie is worth a dozen of her," he said, with his old boyish partiality. "But she is the queerest girl. She always *makes* the nice things come to Ada. She will not see that they are meant for her, and puts them by in that odd fashion that you can't get vexed over, and never seems to miss them when some one else appropriates them without so much as a thank you."

"Is n't that the highest and finest regard for others, — working for them and yet never making them feel the weight of favors ?" asked Jessie, looking into her brother's clear eyes.

"I suppose it is. O dear, how much goodness it does take to make us good, after all !"

Jessie smiled. "And yet I think Kathie *is* rewarded. When we see her do these pleasant things for others, we always try to do the next delightful favor for her. Gruff old Dr. Markham takes as much pains for her as if she were the greatest lady in the land."

"As if she was n't !" exclaimed Charlie, with enthusiasm. "But I like her to accept my small favors for herself, and not be handing them over to others."

"O Charlie, maybe that is a hint that you ought to offer *twice* as many," Jessie returned, laughingly.

"Well, I never thought of that. I do believe I have been a little cross sometimes and held up, so I will take the lesson."

Mr. Meredith could not make a very long stay, as it would not do for both of them to leave the business. They all teased Jessie to spend the remainder of the summer at her old home, but she seemed to think that her husband's claim was first and strongest.

Uncle Robert brought Ada and her trunk over one day in the light wagon. She was to have Aunt Ruth's sleeping apartment. The crimson room with the bay-window had fallen into ordinary use as a sitting-room, and Kathie sewed, studied, and had all her fancy-work here. Not a nook or corner but spoke of Aunt Ruth.

They had heard from the boys in the mean while, who had reached their destination safely, and, if one could judge from the tenor of their letters, were well-nigh transformed into wild Indians themselves. Such rides over plains and prairies, such a scaling of mountains and hunting up of cascades and curious haunts and game of all kinds! General Mackenzie

was a most magnificent uncle, and Aunt Ruth was a
most lovely stepmother.   Only — if Kathie *could* be
there !

She thought of them all as she was beautifying the
room with flowers, and wondered a little if she could
have given up such a pleasure for Ada's sake, feeling
very glad that she had not been asked.

"O, how cool and delightful!" Ada exclaimed.
"What beautiful flowers! There is an odd sweet
home feeling about your house, after all."

"I am glad you think so," Kathie said, pleased
with the late praise.

"Not but what they are very nice over at the
Darrells'. It is quaint and old-fashioned, with their
great rooms and low ceilings and heavy furniture.
Sometimes I think —"

Ada paused so long that Kathie glanced shyly at
her, and found her eyes filled with tears.

"You are all very good," she said, in a tone that
sounded cold and ungracious almost, and yet it was
because her heart had been stirred to its very depths
with a new and unwonted emotion. Love and grati-
tude did not come to her naturally, and the first
awakenings were a little constrained and awkward.

Kathie went over to her presently, and kissed her quietly. Perhaps one great charm in her affection was that it never overwhelmed, was never obtrusive, but as simple and graceful as her own pure self.

CHAPTER VII.

THE ENEMIES' TARES.

"I WONDER what we shall do, or *can* do ?" Kathie said to her mother the next evening, in great perplexity.

It had been a long, quiet day. No one had "run in." Ada had rested and read and looked out of the windows. Kathie had gone up and down and in and out rather restlessly for her, sewed a little and tatted a little.

"About what ?" asked her mother.

"I want to try and entertain Ada, and I don't just know what to do. If Rob were home, or if all the larger girls were not away —"

"It seems to me the most necessary lesson for Ada to learn is to entertain herself."

"But, mamma —"

"Not that you should be indifferent, my dear. Yet a great many of the loveliest lives I have known were made up of common things and trifles. It cannot be one great holiday, and the quicker every one learns this the better."

" But I am afraid Ada cannot understand."

" You must not let your missionary work become a task and a burden. I cannot have my little girl's bright face grave and overclouded."

" But, mamma, is n't it right that one should do everything for a friend, if one wanted to make her happier and — " " Better," Kathie was about to say, but paused, rather distrusting her own powers.

" In one sense, yes ; in another, no. I am not sure that I can quite explain my meaning to you, so we will take Ada for an illustration. All her life she has been waited upon, amused, and had a constant variety in every respect. Rich people can nearly always do this, if they choose. It has made her entirely dependent upon others. Now she cannot have this constant ministering, and perhaps never will in her life again. Is it wise for all her friends to keep up the pretence ? "

" But it is n't comfortable to feel that one is dull."

" No. I should like to see you use all the means within your power, and though there are cases when we go out of our way and take upon ourselves a great deal of arduous perplexity, it does not seem to me that this is one of the instances where it can be rightly demanded. Ada has had very little come to interest her through the winter and spring, and I dare say it never occurred to her that she might go out and find something, use her own dormant energies instead of taxing other people. I think we know of one who made a little heaven below by her unselfish ways, when she had a great deal to suffer and no outside pleasures."

"Oh! Aunt Ruth," Kathie said, with a glad, bright smile.

"Yes, dear Aunt Ruth. Yet she might easily have made herself so unlovely that she would not at all have attracted the notice of a grand and tender gentleman like General Mackenzie, and said, with much show of truth, that she could not help being fretful, dependent, and dissatisfied."

"I wish you would tell me just what to do, mamma," her perplexity not entirely cleared.

"I should go on much as usual, and not give up my own duties and pleasures altogether. Always invite Ada to share them, but not allow her to feel that she has the *right* to change your whole life simply

because she has come into it for a while. You will
have to go on when she drops out of it."

Kathie began to understand. Each person in this
world had certain individual rights which, though
she might relinquish them for a brief while under
peculiar circumstances, were not to be made another's
property through selfishness.

An incident occurred the next morning. Kathie
was up early, and had been down to the Morrison
cottage to see Ethel and grandmother, coming back
with glowing cheeks, as Freddy had bantered her to
run a race up the drive.

Mrs. Alston made no difference with the breakfast
hour, but she did not insist that Ada should be present, since she was in the habit of rising late. It was
only a few minutes' work to get a dainty little meal,
and Jane was willing to do it if Hannah was busy.

Kathie was just sitting down to the table when
Harry Cox ran across the lawn. She went to the
open window.

"O," said Harry, laughingly, "good morning! I
should n't have come so early, but the girls asked me
to do an errand last evening, and I did forget all
about it."

" Won't you walk in and take some breakfast with us ? " asked Mrs. Alston. " You ought to have a good appetite for it."

"O, I had it, — fifteen minutes ago, appetite and all; but thank you all the same. The girls want to come over this afternoon, Kathie, if — you were not going anywhere. And could we have the boat out a while ? "

Kathie glanced at her mother with an odd smile.

" How many ? " asked Mrs. Alston.

"O, Mary and Till, and the Gardiner girls, and Carry Jelliffe, and two or three of us boys. Mary thought it would be nice before — before you had company," exclaimed Harry, blushing.

" Mary and Lucy and Annie were to come to tea. O mamma, can't we have them all ? " and Kathie glanced up entreatingly.

" But the company ? " said Uncle Robert, in a low tone.

Kathie's thoughts recurred to her last evening's conversation. Would it not be rather foolish and selfish to disappoint the gay little party for the sake of one ?

" Well, Kathie ? "

"O mamma, I should like to have them come."

"Very well. Harry, tell them that we shall be very glad to see them all, and that we shall expect them to stay to supper. And you boys as well."

Harry nodded, with graceful satisfaction.

"And come early," appended Kathie. "Give my love to them."

"Now you must tell Hannah as soon as you are through, and decide what it would be nice to have; for I am afraid a little cream and sponge-cake will not be just the thing for a hungry troop."

Before breakfast was ended they had another call. Little Dolly Maybin ran over to see "if Janie might come home to-day. Mother was sick in bed, and Martha had a sore finger."

"It will be rather bad to spare her to-day, still, I suppose she ought to go."

"O yes," said Kathie. "I can help, and there won't be so very much to do."

"If she will come back early."

Jane was in something of a flurry when she heard it. Mrs. Maybin had been ailing for a week or ten days. Threatened with a fever, Jane thought. And if she should have a long illness —

"Never mind; we will not worry until it happens," said Mrs. Alston. "Come back by five, and let us know how she is. Then, after supper is through, you may return."

Kathie ran out to the kitchen. "We are going to have a surprise-party, Hannah," she said, "only they do not bring their eatables along. And Jane has had to go home to her sick mother."

"How large a party?" and Hannah held up her skimmer, as she was improving her spare moments by doing blackberries.

"O, four or five girls, and as many boys maybe. But we don't need to make any great time."

"I was going to do preserves all the morning," said Hannah, who gave the possible objections first and the cheerful willingness afterward.

"I can make the cake and some jelly; and, O mamma, may we have cream? Uncle Robert will see to that, I know."

"Yes, if he chooses. Kathie may as well make the cake this morning, Hannah, but wait until Ada has had her breakfast."

"And the bread and biscuit?" said Hannah. "We had just about enough to last over till to-morrow."

"The biscuits may as well be cold, as they are really better for the children."

"Why, I can make them too. It will seem quite like old times. I have n't done any kitchen work in ever so long."

Kathie cleared the "pastry-table," and began to bring out some materials.

"You had better put your room in order," said her mother, "and then you will have the whole morning."

So Kathie ran up stairs. The bed had been airing in the morning sunshine, so she spread it up and dusted, and brought in a few fresh flowers. At that juncture Ada called.

"I have had such a lovely sleep!" she exclaimed.

I suppose you have been up an hour or two, and you look as bright as a rose. Dear, if I ever *could* look well again! I am getting real sallow, — am I not? — and I did have such a sweet complexion. But it does n't matter, after all. I shall never care much for anything again. O Kathie, if you only *would* do up my back hair! You can always manage it so nicely. Are you going to wear curls forever?"

Kathie's curls were tied in a knot behind with

a blue ribbon, and looked both cool and comfortable.

"I don't know. Why are they not as good as
'boughten ones,' as Fred calls them?"

"But if you would braid part of it—"

"I will wait until I have to," Kathie returned,
laughingly, taking up the comb.

Kathie packed and padded after the requirements
of fashion. She did not wonder that Ada's head often
ached, with the cushion and the rolls and the great
braid that was stuffed inside with just hair enough to
cover the top.

"It is a beautiful morning,— is n't it? Could
not we go out driving, Kathie, before it gets so very
warm?"

"You may. I shall be busy. Uncle Robert will
take you with pleasure."

"What are you going to do?"

"Jane has been sent for; her mother is sick."

"Something is always happening to servants, or to
their fathers and mothers. However, I will excuse
you then"; for she felt that she would full as lief go
with Uncle Robert.

Kathie washed her hands and ran down stairs,

made a little toast and a cup of fresh coffee. Then she sat and chatted with Ada, who did seem in a very gracious mood. But as she heard Uncle Robert's step, she ran out into the hall and preferred her request.

"That just suits me," he said, good-humoredly. "I want to go over to the village."

Ada put on her hat and stepped into the basket phaeton as if it was all her very own, and threw a rose-colored shawl over her light dress for effect, while she played with her inevitable sandal-wood fan, brought from Paris by mamma.

Kathie carried the few dishes out to the kitchen, stood a great vase of flowers on the table, and darkened the blinds a trifle, to give the room a cool, shady look. Then she ran up stairs. Ada always did litter a room so. Here was her night-dress, there her sack, her slippers nearly in the middle of the floor, all her toilet articles about, and yesterday's dress thrown over a chair. She often laughed at Kathie for her old-maidish ways, but the child could not help thinking how much time and trouble orderly habits saved.

It was just nine when she went back to the kitchen.

Hannah was washing dishes between, now, to fill up the vacancy.

"I will have time to make your biscuit," she said.

"O Hannah, if you would only make some of your delightful macaroons instead!"

"Would you like them, — really? Yes, I will do that and anything I can. And we will have the cream all right this afternoon. Children always *do* have such a good time when they come to this house."

Kathie thought so too as she went at the biscuits. Two large pans full, looking absolutely flaky in the dough. Hannah held her hand in the oven a minute. "I guess it won't be too hot. They are beauties, Miss Kathie."

Then she went to beating eggs. Hannah declared that it was too hard, and took the bowl and the beater herself.

"You ought to be a little careful, Miss Kathie, and not spread your hands now while you are growing. Little girls' hands are tender."

Kathie laughed. "Mamma's hands are pretty, and she has done a great deal of work."

"It was after she had her growth. People's bones settle then, and are not so easily strained."

9

Kathie did not take exception in physical or logical view of the case, for beating eggs on a warm day *was* hard work.

Mrs. Alston came in with her bonnet on and parasol in hand. " I am going down to Mrs. Maybin's," she said. " I think, by the appearance of things, you can get along without me. Don't hurry yourself to death, as you will want to be fresh for this afternoon."

" Mamma, shall we not ask Ethel too ? Annie and Lucy like her so much."

" I will stop on my way."

Hannah was quite delighted to have Kathie in the kitchen, and made her tell over the visit to Washington. Then she made some crisp, golden jumbles, set in Kathie's cake, and the work was nearly done. She wanted to see the macaroons made, and was quite sure she could do it herself another time.

She had her face washed and a fresh white dress on when Ada returned. They had a very pleasant drive, of course, but she was almost tired to death. Mr. Langdon crossed the wide porch at that moment, so she did not go up stairs.

" How cool and delightful you look !" he said. I suppose, like Solomon's lilies, you eschew toiling and spinning, this warm weather! I was lazy and lonesome, and have come over to be amused."

"What shall we do, — play croquet?" and a roguish light gleamed in Kathie's eyes.

"It is cruel in you even to hint at a mallet. You had better stay me with music, and comfort me with singing instead."

"As if that was not exertion!"

He laughed.

"I believe you and your friend sing very beautifully together. Suppose you try."

Ada was all out of voice and out of practice, then her health had been so delicate for the last six months that she was sure she had no strength. But after a while she did sing, and that very prettily. Kathie watched her returning animation with pleasure.

"Miss Kathie," he said, as he was going away, "won't you and your friend walk over to Miss Lauriston's this afternoon when it begins to grow shady? I promised to take some books to her brother, and I have exhumed an old art review that I think will interest her."

"I am to have some company to-day. O Mr. Langdon," — with a happy after-thought, — "they

want a sail.   I wish you would take out your boat,
there will be so many of us.   And to-morrow I shall
be glad to go to Emma's."

"With pleasure.   Who are *they?*"

"Some of my old schoolmates."

"Consider me invited.   I like little girls' parties."

"We shall be glad to see you."

"Who is coming?" asked Ada, as she watched
Mr. Langdon cross the lawn.

"Four or five of the girls sent me word this morning."

"Rather a short notice, I should say.   Any one I
have ever seen?"

"The Gardiner girls and — Mary Cox —"

"O, I don't wonder Mr. Langdon said *little* girls.
And country girls are such romps and hoydens."

Kathie colored a trifle.   Ada always managed to
make her feel uncomfortable.

The bell rang for lunch, and Mrs. Alston returned
just in time.   So the party dropped for a moment.

"How is Mrs. Maybin, mamma?"

"Very ill indeed.   She was taken worse last night.
Jane will not be able to come home, so we shall have
to do the best we can without her."

"It is a pity that people have not sense enough to
wait until they are invited," Ada said, when the two
girls were alone. "How *are* you going to manage
with only one servant?"

"O, everything is done but the cream. I helped
Hannah bake this morning. And Uncle Robert is
always so kind. Besides, it seems to me that there
is a great deal of true enjoyment in these little in-
formal parties."

"But you have to work so hard."

"If you make others happy you feel amply repaid."

"I should not," in a rather dry, hard tone. "I
should be too tired even to think."

"But if everybody in the world felt the same way!
If no one was willing to do anything because it was
a trouble, or —"

Kathie was a little astonished at her sudden burst
of frankness, and was afraid for the moment that she
had vexed Ada by reflection.

But there was no reply made. Ada looked a shade
more thoughtful, not displeased.

She put on a wrapper and went to bed, for she was
really tired, and after fanning herself awhile she fell
asleep.

Kathie went to look after Uncle Robert and the cream, and they had quite a merry time.

"I am going to set the table now," said Hannah, "so there won't be everything to do in a hurry, for I can't get along as spry as Jane. And she won't be quite so frisky when she begins to go down the other side."

The girls came early, of course. They wanted a good time and oceans of fun. There were Mary and her cousin Tilly Waite, the Gardiners and *their* cousin, a tall, good-looking fellow, who was actually a banking-clerk, and Carry Jelliffe. Harry Cox had hunted up Charlie Darrell.

The glad and rather boisterous voices roused Ada.

"As if any one cared to be among those snips!" she said disdainfully to herself, and shut up her eyes again, never so much as winking when Kathie came in to look at her.

"It is good to see you once more," began Mary. "But, O Kathie, we had no idea that Miss Meredith was here! Why, I had half a mind to turn back with my lords of Spain when I heard it. Must we all be proper and formal, and put on our Sunday manners?"

"Let me catch you at it!" exclaimed Mr. Langdon, bringing up the rear with Dick Grayson. "Here we are, two jolly boatmen, at your service, and the first one who does n't laugh as often as once in five minutes will be fined. Proceeds to go towards cakes and cream."

They all looked desperately sober, half frightened in fact, and then began to smile until it almost settled into a giggle.

"Will you have the sail first? There is a nice shady side to the lake."

"O Mr. Langdon, we did not expect so much attention," exclaimed Mary. "How good you are, Kathie!"

"Don't give her the credit. I invited myself."

"As we all did. Does n't your mother think us ridiculous, Kathie? We only meant to come over and take a sail and have a game of croquet —"

Mrs. Alston came out on the porch and welcomed them cordially, and Dick made a neat little speech in return.

"Where is Ada?" asked Uncle Robert, joining them.

"She was tired and went to lie down," Kathie said,

softly. "Mamma, will you please look after her a little when she wakes?"

"Come, rank and file, fall into line. My bark rocks in the tide. Is n't that poetical, girls? Miss Kathie, are you the admiral? if so, lead the party."

The girls laughed a little and paired off. Uncle Robert took shy Ethel under his wing. There seemed no likelihood of any one being fined just yet, for each one added a sentence that kept the ball rolling.

Down the wide walk they went gayly enough. Ada rose and glanced out of the window after them. Why, she never supposed there would be gentlemen enough to go round. Uncle Robert, Mr. Langdon, Dick, and another tall youth, beside Charlie and Harry. Why had n't she opened her eyes when Kathie came in, and been coaxed to accompany them! It showed plainly enough that Kathie did not care anything special for her. And she had promised to stay a month; perhaps Kathie would go on neglecting her in this fashion, and she would be miserable and homesick. O dear, she might as well die! No one cared for her, no one took any trouble to please her, and, burying her face on the pillow, she sobbed as if her heart was breaking.

Out on the lake they had the gayest madcap time, singing, shouting, and laughing. It takes so little to amuse healthy, happy young people, who have not yet grown worldly-wise. And somehow, Mr. Langdon seemed to be in a great glee, as if he had come back to boyish moods and days.

"We ought to return now," said Kathie, at length, thinking of Ada. She did not want any one to feel neglected.

CHAPTER VIII.

THE ONE TALENT.

"Are you awake?" said a clear, sweet voice. "I came in just before we started, and you were sleeping beautifully. We have had such a lovely sail, and I am so sorry you did not go. Are you rested, and shall I help you dress?"

Ada knew it had been her own fault. With Kathie's brave, honest eyes upon her, she could not evade the truth, and she had a misgiving that it would be rather foolish to stay alone the remainder of the afternoon and evening.

"I will try to help myself," she answered, rather condemned for her selfish tears. "They will want you."

"One set is playing croquet, and the other resting. No, let me help you; it will be done so much the sooner."

The beautiful puff and rolls had to be taken down, and the crimps showed the effects of the warm weather

somewhat. Kathie's nimble fingers soon had them in
order. She had brought up a spray of old-fashioned
button-roses and wreathed them in, and gave her another cluster for her bosom.

"You have improved since you came to Brookside,"
said Kathie, confidently.

Ada had a little color now, though it was partly
shame, and the haughtiness was a trifle subdued.

Kathie led her right into the midst of the group.
To be sure, all the girls were younger, and none of
them actually set up for young ladies. They were
not too old nor too grand to have a good time, if one
might judge from the merry laughter. Mr. Langdon
and Mr. Conover appeared to enjoy the fun as much
as the others.

"Oh!" Mary Cox said, falling back so that Kathie
only could hear. "I did n't know Miss Meredith had
really come to Cedarwood. And I am afraid — "

"No," returned Kathie, with a hurried breath, "it
will not make any difference. You are to go on just
the same."

Mary's cousin Tilly and Carry Jelliffe stood in no
awe of the stranger, and went straight on with the
playing, but the other girls could not so easily shake

off the influence. However, in a few moments a
diversion was made. Fred and Emma Lauriston
came slowly up the walk.

"Why, I did not dream you were having a party,"
Emma exclaimed, in surprise.

"Quite an impromptu affair," explained Uncle
Robert. "You are just in time for supper."

Kathie ran in to announce the new arrivals.

"'It never rains, but it pours' in this house," said
Hannah. "Well, we have a plenty for them all.
Two more plates and cups, and it will be ready.
Only I can't wait on the table as spry as Jane."

"I will help if you get behindhand," returned Kathie, cheerfully.

So the crowd was summoned to the supper-room,
where everything looked cool and neat and lovely,
without any attempt at display. Mrs. Alston poured
the tea, and Hannah carried it round. Mr. Langdon,
Uncle Robert, and Kathie were so distributed that
the serving could be expeditious and not onerous.
The quiet elegance puzzled Ada. How could their
cook have managed such a party alone ? And these
country boys and girls were really very well bred.
Fred Lauriston sat next to her, and was as attentive

to her little wants as any city cavalier. He kept up
quite a conversation on the topics of the day, of
which Ada began to feel dreadfully ignorant by and
by. Of course she might reasonably be excused from
knowing the merits of the different English and
American translations, since Latin and Greek are
hobbies with college boys; but she found that she
could hardly remember a picture, and who had
painted it, and the last winter's lecturers were like
so many Egyptian mummies in the chaos of her
mind, all alike.

"I was ill last winter, and did not go out at all,"
she confessed, at length.

"What a pity! For, after all, Miss Meredith,
there is n't anything like health. I believe I have
been rather prodigal of mine, but henceforward I
mean to be the most careful of the careful. There
is so much to do in the world, so much to learn, and
O, so very much to enjoy!"

"Is there?" said Ada, doubtingly. She wanted to
add, "If one can only be rich," but an inward feeling
restrained her.

"Don't you find it so?" with a glance of surprise.
"Why, the whole world is full of beauty and pleasant

people, and so many charming little events happening
constantly, and a new hope for next week or next
year, — yes, I do think it delightful to live and to
add one's little mite to the general fund."

"But if one does not have even a mite?" she returned, hesitatingly.

"O, everybody must have. You know even the
unprofitable servant had *one* talent given to him.
And if we go on cultivating the one quality it seems
to branch out like a tree, and give a little fragrance
or a little shade to some one standing near. We can
never tell just what it will do until we try."

Ada did not reply immediately. If Aunt Jessie or
Dr. Markham had said this she would have called it
grown-up preaching, or it would not have astonished
her in Kathie; but that any young man should take
life so seriously amazed her.

Then Mr. Langdon spoke to him. The younger
boys had broken out into a base-ball discussion.
Fred seemed to know as much about this as the
Latin, and as much about boating as either. He was
no prig, but a very thorough big boy, and a gentlemanly one as well.

How happy they all were! Ada fairly envied

them. Heretofore she had rather disdained simple enjoyments, but what if she was never to have operas and balls and fashionable watering-places in her life again? Of course, these children knew of nothing better.

They went out on the lawn for another game of croquet. Kathie was drawn into it, but the elders stood apart in a group and had some pleasant conversation. Mr. Langdon was questioning Emma about her further pursuit of art, and mentioning some books he would like to send her. Why, even she, educated in an ordinary country school, knew more than Ada. Not that Mr. Langdon was talking very learnedly. On the contrary it was a simple, pleasant chat, and, in spite of her rather supercilious mood, Ada could not help being interested, and found herself wishing that she did know somewhat of these matters, instead of the glimmering chaos that seemed to float through her brain.

"Now we ought to wind up with a good sing," said Charlie Darrell, gathering the mallets, while Uncle Robert picked up the balls.

"I will second that," declared Fred and Mr. Langdon in a breath.

"To the parlor then," said Uncle Robert.

The low windows were wide open, and the room was fragrant with heliotrope and mignonette. The crowd rushed up the steps in gay good-humor, and not as noisily as one might have imagined.

"Who will play ? "

"Oh ! Emma, or Kathie, or — "

"Emma knows the songs we all sing."

Uncle Robert went to her and held out his hand with a smile.

"I will play first," she said, with a touch of simple grace, "and then I want Kathie and Miss Meredith to sing a chorus that I think so beautiful."

So she gave them a familiar song, all the voices joining in the refrain. Bright, joyous voices they were, and the glad faces were a picture in themselves.

Ada had to be coaxed quite a good deal afterward. She honestly felt her inability, for she had lost much of her proficiency through these months of listlessness. However, she acquitted herself very creditably, after a little awkwardness at first.

"It is exceedingly beautiful," said Mr. Langdon, as she half turned to leave the circle. "I want you to

sing again before the evening is over, so I am going
to take you to a quiet corner and let you rest. You
have that richest of all voices, Miss Meredith, a contralto, only you do not seem strong enough to manage it."

Ada had been complimented a great many times,
and taken it quite as a right, but the friendliness and
appreciation of this went to her heart.

Mr. Langdon led her to a corner and seated her
comfortably, then took the opposite chair.

"Why, you are really tired," he said, for he discerned the nervous flutter in every pulse. "You
need a month or two of our healthful country air.
I think you were wise to come to Brookside instead
of trying fashionable dissipation."

"I have been an invalid all winter," she returned,
languidly.

"I don't know how you girls manage to lose your
roses and your health, unless it is that fashion decrees
health to be vulgar. Yet to all sensible men and
women nothing is more enchanting than perfect
health and spirits. Look at those faces."

They all looked so pretty and vivacious that Ada
could hardly criticise in her usual carping fashion.

10

Perhaps, too, she was rather desirous of Mr. Langdon's good opinion.

" And you gave up the music, I suppose," he said, presently.

" I was not well enough to practise, and — there was no one to — help me keep up the interest. Papa lost his fortune, and there was a great change in our lives."

" And you lost hope, courage, health, — is that it ? " He smiled in so pleasant a manner that she could not take offence.

" It was a great shock to us all, giving up the things we cared most for."

" Was not the mistake just there, Miss Meredith ? I am not one to undervalue wealth, but is it the chief good ? Can we have nothing pleasant without it ? "

Ada glanced around with a kind of tacit reproach in her face.

" Yes, I know what you are thinking of, Miss Meredith, — that, without the aid of wealth, this scene would lose half its brightness. Much would be taken away, I grant, yet I have a fancy that Miss Kathie learned the true secret of life and happiness in poverty. I like to watch her now, and I do not know two women whom I admire as much as her mother and her aunt. But their chief pleasure appears to be in distributing, not hoarding."

Ada looked a little perplexed, as if she did not clearly understand.

'There is that which withholdeth, and yet maketh poor," he continued, with a smile. " Many of the good things of this world increase with the using. All that we give out of our own heart enriches, and if we treat it like a miser's treasure, it seems to decrease daily. I think this house ought to be called the Palace Bountiful, for every one is taken in and treated to the best, not mere odds and ends. And that is the charm of the hospitality. Look at Kathie now. Who shall say that she is not twice blest in giving."

She did certainly look very radiant, making a laughing reply after the song was done.

" I believe we all like to come here, old and young, and we go away satisfied. Yet many people in the world offer grander feasts. I think it is the sweet, ungrudging cordiality, the desire that every one, no matter how humble, shall share the best."

Was that the secret of it, and Kathie's success as well ? For every one *was* attracted toward her. Uncle Edward had been won instantly, and there were General Mackenzie and queer old Dr. Markham, who thought there never could be another Kathie while the world stood. These praises had often given Ada a jealous pang. Yet no one in their whole circle " sought her own " less than Kathie, and to no one was so much freely given.

" Now we will leave Kathie and come back to you," he began again, with an odd smile. " Are you going to give up the charms and graces that add so much to women's lives ? "

" What charms ? " Ada asked, her vanity a little wounded.

" Well, music for one. So many girls let it drop with their school-days. The world, or society rather, makes so many demands upon them that something must get crowded out or thrust aside. And it is sad to see those gifts and graces relinquished which would render home the happiest for fathers and brothers. Be honest, Miss Meredith, and confess that you think a prosy chap like me would make an excellent father for a great house full of girls."

Ada laughed at the ridiculous idea. A year ago she might have considered him prosy, contrasting him with Saratoga exquisites ; but he appeared exceedingly entertaining now.

"I have no one to practise with," she said, in answer.

"But some one to sing to, I dare say. It is a pity to give up the pleasure of so fine a voice."

"O yes, a quadrille, by all means. Uncle Robert and Mr. Langdon will dance, I know. There will be just enough for two," exclaimed Kathie, in the gayest of tones.

Uncle Robert counted noses.

"Some one must play, unless we depute that to the music-box."

Mrs. Alston offered herself as a substitute. She had helped Hannah take the tea-dishes out to the kitchen, and, instead of grumbling, the willing domestic had insisted upon doing all the rest.

Fred Lauriston insisted that he could not dance, and Harry Cox made them laugh by declaring that he went through the figures with the grace of an elephant and the agility of a two-story Shanghai. However, Uncle Robert promised to call off, and nearly everybody knew the Lancers by heart.

Mr. Langdon led out Ada, and Uncle Robert took Annie Gardiner in charge, who was quite elated. They all danced in such earnest that Ada absolutely caught the infection. Now and then some one blundered and laughed over it, or gave the wrong hand, but they were all merry enough.

Afterward Dick asked Ada to dance with him, and then Edmund Gardiner begged the favor. And though there was little complimenting, there were a good many pleasant and honest things said, which was much better.

So they danced till they were warm and tired. Mr. Langdon had a talk with Emma Lauriston, and Ada was quite sure he had forgotten all about the song. Then the Gardiners thought they *must* go home, and Mary said it was time for them to start, as well.

" We have had the very loveliest time there could possibly be! We always *do* have such a good time when we come here ! " declared enthusiastic Mary.

Kathie was very glad. She kissed them a cordial good-night down on the lawn path, and when she went back Ada was singing for Mr. Langdon, while Dick and Fred were a most attentive audience. Indeed, they sat up much later than usual.

"I did not suppose it would be half so pleasant," Ada said afterward, "for, as a general thing, such children are unendurable."

"There were only two younger than I am," Kathie answered, with a smile.

"O, you know what I mean. Country children do not seem to grow up so soon. How nice Fred Lauriston is, and Dick Grayson always was a gentleman. But Mr. Langdon is charming. And how lovely you did get along with the supper and the serving. I am afraid mamma would have thought my having such a company an awful bother and nuisance."

"But we did not go much out of the ordinary course, you see, and that made it less trouble. Then I helped with the baking this morning, so that Hannah should not be all tired out before supper-time."

"You!" Ada exclaimed, in astonishment.

"It was my company, you know, and Jane had to be away."

"But I should have thought — you would have wanted to be fresh for to-night," was the slow reply.

"And was n't I fresh?"

She looked as bright as a pink now, although it

was past eleven. And how ready, how generous she
had been with herself and all her surroundings! Yes,
there was some rich, hidden stream that kept the
banks always overflowing and always blooming.

It was late, as usual, when Ada came down the
next morning. Kathie brought in the *tête-à-tête*
breakfast.

It occurred to Ada then that she was making a
good deal of needless trouble. So long as there was
a servant to do it, she felt no compunctions of conscience. Servants were paid for it, and it was no
matter how much one gave them to do. But to-
morrow she would really try. Perhaps the resolve
was stronger for being made in the quiet of her own
soul. Then she went into the parlor and practised
for an hour. When she returned to her own room
everything was in the neatest order.

"Who takes care of the chambers now that Jane
is away?" she asked of Kathie.

The child blushed with sudden embarrassment.

"Mamma does hers, and I mine."

"And mine?"

Kathie's color deepened.

"I am sorry to make you so much extra work."

"O Ada, you need not be *sorry*. It is a pleasure to do what you can for another, and I wanted you to come. It is unfortunate that Jane should be away just at this time, but I find plenty of leisure for little things like that. And if you care at all for me, you will enjoy it, and not think yourself a trouble."

"You *are* good, Kathie. I wish I could make amends."

"You did last night," was the eager reply. "I was glad to see you talk to Mr. Langdon, and to have you sing and act so graciously towards the others, who were nearly strangers to you."

"They were all very kind to me."

"Because you were pleasant with them. It is always so"; and an eager light trembled in the child eyes, as if there was a host of things left unsaid which she was longing to utter.

The ponies came prancing up under the window, and Kathie looked out.

"Will you and Ada drive now?" asked Uncle Robert. "Fred and I have had a very delightful time."

"Yes, we will soon be ready. I think we shall not find it too warm, Ada. The sun is partly under a cloud."

" I shall enjoy it, I know."

Ada drove. She was beginning to feel much interested in the amusement.

" How good of your uncle to take Fred Lauriston out! I believe you are the most generous people that I ever knew. You don't think Mr. Lauriston really ill, do you ? "

" Uncle Robert believes that it is only the result of overwork. He has been taking care of himself in college, teaching and doing whatever he could. He gave up his vacation entirely last summer."

" Why does not his sister help him ? Is n't she an heiress ? "

" Will be " ; and Kathie smiled thoughtfully. " She only has a small amount every year until she is twenty-one, and the rest she cannot touch."

" Why does she wish to go on studying or painting then, if she will have enough by and by ? "

" She likes it. And Mrs. Wilder thought she had a good deal of genius. So does Mr. Langdon. She means to be an artist sometime."

" And I suppose you will be — something or other — " said Ada, with a touch of secret dissatisfaction.

" No, I do not believe I shall have a bit of genius

of any kind," Kathie answered, with thorough content in her voice. "I shall just be commonplace, but I mean to be — the nicest commonplace there is"; and the dimpled lips broke into a sweet smile.

They drove along slowly and in silence. After a long while Ada spoke again. "I wonder — if I could ever do anything with my voice. It has changed some, you see, and Mr. Langdon said last night that, when properly trained, a contralto voice was the richest of all. But a musical education would cost a good deal, and there it is again." Ada's eyes filled with tears, though Kathie tried to comfort her.

CHAPTER IX.

FIRST THE LEAVES.

WHEN Ada heard the bell the following morning, she roused herself with less effort than she supposed would be necessary. It rang at half past six, and gave an hour before breakfast-time. She heard Kathie trip softly down stairs, and then made for herself a simple toilet, without the elaborate braids and puffs. To her great surprise she found she had full fifteen minutes left. This she spent in picking up her stray ribbons, slippers, and sundry parts of dresses, making the room quite tidy. Then she spread the sheets over a chair in the morning sunshine, as she had noticed Kathie always did.

Freddy was trudging up stairs to put away some lost playthings.

"Why, you look — as sweet — as a rose!" he exclaimed, with the utmost deliberation.

"Thank you for the compliment," she returned.

laughingly. Somehow she did feel unusually fresh and bright.

They all had a pleasant word of welcome. Kathie pushed her small bouquet over to Ada's plate.

"I should have made another if I had guessed you were coming," she said, with cordial sweetness.

How cool and neat and pretty everything looked! There were no noisy children to pull the cloth about and clatter their forks and plates. And yet *their* children use to behave nicely when they had a nursery by themselves. What was the reason that everything went wrong now? Ada felt at the moment as if she would fain stay away from home forever.

Kathie wanted to cut fresh flowers for the house, so Ada went out in the garden with her. What a lovely profusion of everything! They filled a great basket, and you could not miss them.

Ada entered the spacious clean kitchen. There did not seem the usual steamy smell of cooking, and very few articles were littered around. Hannah was by the sink-table washing dishes, and presented a striking contrast to their frowzy-headed Bridgets.

Kathie washed the vases and refilled them, and made two or three loose pyramids in glass dishes.

"What are you going to do with these?" asked Ada, when everything had been replenished.

"Send them over to Mrs. Maybin. Mamma is going presently."

"All those beautiful flowers!" Ada exclaimed, involuntarily.

"Flowers are like the man who was 'counted mad,'" returned Kathie, laughingly. "'The more he gave away, the more he had,' you know. O Hannah, did you make this wine-jelly?"

"No, miss; your mamma did it. And the custard will soon be done."

"So there is nothing left for me then. Ada, will you help carry the flowers through?"

Kathie dusted the parlor; the library and dining-room had been put in order before breakfast. Then the two girls went up stairs.

Ada tried spreading up her bed. It was quite an art, after all, not to have the covering askew, and the pillows straight. On the whole, she felt rather proud of her exploit.

"Oh!" Kathie exclaimed, in surprise.

"You did not suppose that I could do anything of the kind, did you? And I am not at all tired. Why,

I begin to feel as if I might get entirely well. Only it seems so different here."

"Everybody has to help, in order to make their lives different from what they have been," Kathie said, with sweet gravity. "Nothing in this world seems to happen of itself. But you came here to recruit, so you must not begin too hard."

"I am sure that was not tiresome. And it is not nine yet. Are we going out this morning?"

"I don't know. There are so many budgets that Uncle Robert will have to drive mamma over to Mrs. Maybin's. And O, he has brought Emma and Fred home with him!"

Sure enough. Emma looking like a princess in her simple white piqué dress, and her hat finished with black lace and a cluster of rosebuds.

She, too, remarked Ada's improvement. They sat on the shady porch and sewed, while Fred, with his face among the greenery, talked to them. Mr. Langdon came in, and, after a music practice, they had a cosey lunch.

"We will take the cool of the afternoon for our drive," Kathie said. "You were up so early that you had better lie down and have a little rest."

Ada did begin to feel tired.   She was so little used
to any exertion, that, in spite of the enjoyment, it
exhausted her.   Yet, somehow, she was not sleepy,
and her brain kept in a whirl and tangle of thought.
For the first time in her life she had a consciousness
of something truly better than had hitherto filled up
her months and years.   How happy and satisfied
most of these people appeared!   They did not disdain the trifling every-day round, but brought to
every hour's work some joy and pleasure.   Their
toils did not make them coarse, nor common, nor
ignorant.   Emma Lauriston would be none the less
a lady anywhere because she helped her grandmother
in their simple housework.   And no one despised
Kathie for her quaint household knowledge.

But was there not something back of it all, — a grace
or earnestness or humility that she did not possess,
an underlying motive higher than any that had ever
ruled her or the little world in which she had dwelt
until recently?   And if there was more than she had
been educated to believe, if one's duty was more to
one's neighbor and less to one's self, if it was the
giving out that brought sweetest delight, and not
the perpetual self-aggrandizement —   And there she
seemed lost in her mental wanderings.

On the whole, perhaps it was well for the success of Kathie's experiment that Jane Maybin had been compelled to leave her post for a while. There were necessarily more demands upon Kathie, and though Ada would hardly have considered a servant's comfort and convenience, it did appear selfish to be waited upon continually by her friend. It was her first lesson in helping herself, as well as in thinking for others. It was less difficult, because there were so few demands upon her time. Dressing was not made the grand end and aim of existence here ; yet no one, not even the most ordinary of Kathie's acquaintances, displayed any positive neglect. And Ada could not help admitting to herself that there was as much good-breeding here, if they had not all the touches of city elegance.

Fred and Emma fell into the habit of being almost constant visitors. It was so pleasant over here with the large lawn and shady nooks, Uncle Robert, and Mrs. Alston's sweet motherly ways. All big boys seemed nearer to her for Rob's sake. They talked over the gay summer of the boat-club and the races, played chess, backgammon, and croquet, and had amateur concerts. Charlie Darrell and Dick went

11

away for a fortnight, but Mr. Langdon promised to come twice as often to fill their places.

Then there were some delightful readings, in which the gentlemen took turns, or the whole party tried their best at Shakespeare. Emma and Ada went over their French and Italian with Mr. Langdon for tutor. Ada began to regret her utter waste of the past year when she saw how much she had lost. There *was* something still left to life, even if the riches had taken wings.

"Here is a note from Middleville," said Uncle Robert one morning. "Why, we have almost lost sight of Sarah."

Kathie broke the seal. Quite a lengthy epistle indeed. Sarah had been away, making a visit at her grandmother's, and, most wonderful to relate, actually had a situation in a school offered to her.

"Grandmother thought my going to school such folly," she wrote, "and insisted that father was throwing away his money, and I wasting my time ; but was n't she surprised when this happened ? It was an assistant's position, with a salary of three hundred dollars a year, and grandmother offered to give me my board for what I could do nights and mornings, and

would have felt really proud if I had taken it. Indeed, she could not help telling all the neighbors and
making a great time. But father said I was too
young, and that he could not spare me; but I know
he was pleased at my being asked. So I have no
fear about finding a situation when I do want one."

Kathie read this aloud. "Was n't it delightful
and encouraging?" she said, enjoying it as much as
if some good fortune had happened to herself. "For
Sarah has tried her utmost, and there were many
discouragements."

"She has proved herself a brave, persevering girl,"
replied Mrs. Alston.

There was much beside this. Sarah was extremely
anxious to see Kathie, and begged her to come up
and spend a day. She had so many things to tell
her and to ask her about.

"Why do you not go?" asked Ada. "I will cheerfully relinquish my right in you one day at least."

"Will you?" and she smiled.

"I will promise to take very good care of Ada,"
said Mrs. Alston.

Jane was coming back the next week. Her mother was recovering, and had gone away for a few days'

change of air. Jane had remained to keep house
and look after the children, and the knowledge she
had acquired under Mrs. Alston's guidance stood her
in good stead. For Mrs. Alston had not considered
the duties all on one side, but was helping to train
this young girl rightly, that she might occupy a
useful sphere.

They were quite relieved to have the household go
on in its olden fashion. Yet Ada felt that she had
learned a serviceable lesson. She no longer scattered
her garments and small belongings broadcast. It was
possible to be of use to one's self.

"If you would not mind, I think I ought to go to
Sarah for a day," Kathie confessed, after some consideration. "I wish you and Uncle Robert would drive
up in the afternoon for me. The Strongs are not even
stylish country people, but they are good-hearted and
generous."

Ada had heard a good deal of the story by fragments when it had scarcely interested her. The idea
of taking up an ignorant, uncouth girl, to whom Kathie owed no sort of duty or affection, had appeared
rather ridiculous to her. And yet what fruit it had
borne! She felt how much she had changed when

she could tolerate the grace of this with something more than complacency. There was a better purpose to life than mere selfish aims for one's own enjoyment. " I will come, with pleasure," she made answer.

They started quite early, and took Fred Lauriston along for the drive. He was beginning to improve rapidly now. Mrs. Strong made them come in and have a nice dish of berries and some cake, for she was sure they must be hungry. They were all thoroughly delighted to see Kathie.

Sarah was changing and maturing very rapidly. She had learned how to care for herself without running into the foolish extreme of vanity. She had grown much taller, which made her look less stout, and her abundant hair was smooth and neatly arranged. A good, strong, truthful, honest-hearted woman she would make, inspiring others with her faith and earnestness, and doing her whole duty in whatever state of life she might be called, making her influence felt the more because her work would always speak for her.

It seemed so odd to Kathie that a few pleasant words and a little civility should have led to so great a result.

" I don't know," she said, as Sarah was talking over
the old time when they had first met. " It might all
have come about without any help from me. I am
sure you had all the necessary qualities. I did not
give you those "; and she smiled.

" But I never could have put them together myself.
I used to be full of hungry wants, but I never knew
quite what they were. And now, when I meet with
other people who are no more able to find the way
out alone than I was, I see just what they need. If
I could help somebody else — "

It was the true seed. Not the blossoming and
bearing of fruit for one's own self, but the putting
of something pleasant into a neighbor's garden.

" I am sure you do and will," Kathie returned,
warmly. " There is generally some work or deed
right within our reach."

" And that I have learned from you "; with her
bright smile. " I wonder if people do not often make
mistakes, looking so far off for something to do."

There was all the visit to be told over, and the
plans for the future.

" I have fully resolved to teach, for a while at
least," Sarah declared, with a touch of girlish pride.

" After this year I shall be capable of taking a school, and mother will not need me at home, since there are so many more to grow up."

Would Ada call this another case of working where there was no need ? Kathie smiled to herself.

" Father is afraid that I shall forget all my house-keeping," Sarah went on, laughingly, " but I believe I like it better than I used to. There are so many more meanings to all the common every-day things when you get so that you can understand them. And though it would seem delightful to have all the beau-tiful surroundings and luxuries, and leisure to im-prove and enjoy them, perhaps our lives would not be quite so useful."

" And when we have found out the great purposes of our lives we can be content to do, as well as to enjoy," Kathie returned, with sweet seriousness.

Cousin Nelly and her little boy were still at the Strongs, sheltered by the kindly hearts that did not look upon their deed as any specially charitable work, and gave generously of the best they had. Willie would never miss a father's home or tender care, and what Mrs. Gilbert gave her country would be made up to her as far as human love could do it.

Ada meanwhile had a rather quiet day. Most
of the morning she spent at her music, but after
lunch she sat on the shady balcony with Mrs. Alston, reading and thinking while the latter sewed.
Now and then she glanced up at the pleasant, gracious woman, whose serene face showed no marks of
care or trouble. And yet there must have been many
weary years to her life. How could she have over-
lived everything so entirely?

Mrs. Alston glanced up presently, and caught the
perplexed look. "My dear," she said, "I believe I
have been quite forgetful of Kathie's injunction to
entertain you."

Ada colored a trifle.

"I am sure I ought not to be a burden on every
one," she answered. "I ought to be sufficient for
myself occasionally."

"It is a grand lesson to learn"; and the smile was
very sweet and motherly.

"I am afraid I have not learned many of the grand
lessons," she said, with a humility quite new to her.

"It is not too late."

Something in the tone invited confidence. When
she and Kathie came to the undercurrents there al-

ways seemed to be a feeling of shame holding her back, since she had been the one to rule and patronize. And in this respect she felt more real freedom with Mrs. Alston, or at least as if it was possible to go to her for advice.

"I wish I knew — what to do," she went on, blush-ing and hesitating.

"In what respect?"

"To keep myself from going back to the listless, lonesome life of ever so long. It seems so easy to have interest and entertainment here; but when I get home again — "

"And that is the place of all others where one's interest should centre."

"But there does not seem anything for me to do or enjoy. I can have none of the things that I like best. Our servants are careless, and there are so few friends — "

"My dear young friend," said Mrs. Alston, filling the pause, "let me offer you a suggestion here. I have been through with the same experience, and made some sad mistakes, though I was much older than you. I think we are unjust to our friends when we take it for granted that the only liking they have for us is on account of our wealth. If you were rich, and any young girl in your circle should lose her fortune, would you banish her at once?"

Ada was silent. A year ago she would have done so without any remorse, but she felt now how unjust it would have been.

"I think there are some noble and loyal people in the world, who cannot be turned about by the glitter of gold, though I grant that many do forsake us. But this is what I meant more particularly. When Mr. Alston died, and reverses overtook me, I too believed that my friends would not care for me. I am afraid I was rather cold to their proffered sympathy. I took no pains to keep their regard. To be sure, I had my children and a great many cares, which in some degree excused me; but I have learned since that I made my path more desolate than I had any real need of, and wounded my friends beside."

"But no one has cared for me," said Ada, despondingly.

"No one? Are you quite sure?"

She bethought herself a moment. Uncle Edward and his wife had tried to win her from her nervous depression by offering her many pleasures, and queer old Dr. Markham had taken unusual pains to put some bright things in her way. And there *had* been invitations out, but she could have nothing new to wear, and no carriage to go in, and —

"But how *can* people make themselves happy and satisfied when they are not?" Ada said, vehemently.

"It is a very hard thing, and does not come all at once. The lesson is, 'In whatsoever station we are, therewith to be content.'"

"But you cannot. I was not content last winter."

"Was not that more like apathy and despair than content? I often think this word is misunderstood. I should say extract all the happiness you can from your surroundings, not forgetting to press on to something higher and better; for a barren life is a literal living death. What do you suppose we were placed in the world for, Ada?"

She had never thought much of that, you could tell by the blank look in her face.

"God meant us to do something, or he would not have given us such a variety of faculties, desires, and affections, and then placed duties to correspond. It is to bear some fruit, to perfect some work, so that at the last we shall have something better than the mere leaves, which are never the true end and aim."

"But I can do nothing. I have not had any of the right kind of training, Mrs. Alston. I don't know where to begin."

"That is the rock on which so many young girls are wrecked. They make many spasmodic attempts, and perhaps bring forth a cluster of leaves, but no fruit. Then they are discouraged. It is the misfortune of undertaking too many general things, and no one specific duty. It seems to me, in a home like yours, there is a great deal that a grown-up daughter could do."

"I have no faculty for sewing."

"Do you not suppose you could learn? It seems to me that every woman ought to know enough to wait upon herself in case of an emergency. I suppose that at home you leave everything for the servant to do."

"But she is paid for that," Ada returned, in some surprise.

"You take her time for so much compensation, but, after all, she has only one pair of hands. She has to hurry through with one thing to go at the next. Suppose there were certain things about your own room or your own clothing that you undertook. You would have more leisure and could do it better, doubtless, after a little practice."

Ada was thoughtful and silent. They had fallen into careless habits at home, because the upper servant found her hands pretty full in being nurse, chambermaid, and ordinary seamstress. Buttons and strings were always off, the parlor went undusted, and dozens of petty things that might have been comforts were positive trials.

"And is there no one you could make happier?"

Her mother was not such a woman as Mrs. Alston. Ada doubted in her heart if she could understand or in any way acknowledge the small sweet courtesies that won so bright a smile from Mrs. Alston or Uncle Robert. And the children — But then she did not like children, and Kathie did. There was papa— She remembered now how tired and worn he sometimes looked. Could she do anything for him? Slowly awakening conscience told her that she might try at least.

"And there is your own health, my dear child.

You see now how easy it is, with no positive disease, to fall into the most helpless of invalid habits through sheer inaction. There must be work and interest to every life ; those are inexorable conditions, or the life ceases to be what God designed, and is wrenched from its true purpose, becomes stunted and fruit- less. So that if you make it a simple question of health even, you see how much is lost by frittering it away."

"But I don't love to work. It is hard and unpleas- ant to me."

"There is no necessity for your beginning at the drudgery end"; and Mrs. Alston smiled. "There are so many light and simple deeds that seem like matters of mere courtesy, and yet are some of the sweetest proofs we can offer another of our love. But the true secret lies behind all this. As God has loved us we are to love one another, and he renounced the best of all for our sakes. Can we not give up a little of self for his ?"

Ada seemed so far away from this knowledge. She had gone to church occasionally, and the family called themselves Christian people, but how seldom had God entered into any of their ways or thoughts.

Was it this that made so great a difference between them ?

She had been used to thinking of religion as a gloomy and austere thing. Her mother, too, had sneered a little at Uncle Edward's becoming so over-pious, as she termed it. But he had acted nobly, it must be confessed, and all these people led lives a hundred times more satisfying than hers. She sighed over her perplexity, that was not yet cleared up, but she did half resolve to try if she could better her own vapid, profitless life. At least, henceforward she would not refuse through pride any good thing that might come into it.

Uncle Robert and Mr. Langdon walked up the path, and in a few moments the carriage came round.

"I thought you were not going until after tea," Mrs. Alston exclaimed.

"O yes ; I promised this morning, if Miss Ada would not mind. Kathie desired it so much."

"I believe I shall like it," Ada answered, with a smile, and she went for her hat.

"Kathie's leaven begins to work," Uncle Robert said, with a smile. "If Ada could develop into anything really noble, Meredith would be more than delighted. He thinks he owes his best lesson to our darling."

"I believe I have always had a little prejudice against Ada, but I am sincerely glad to do anything for her, or to have Kathie."

CHAPTER X.

GLEAMS BY THE WAY.

MR. LANGDON rode over to the Lauristons' with them. They caught a glimpse of Emma at the window, and the fair face flushed rosily as he sprang out.

A curious feeling came over Ada Meredith. The interest Mr. Langdon had evinced in her music, and the odd little snatches of talk that he occasionally fell into, had given her a peculiar interest in him. Dick and Charlie and Fred listened and complimented and played games with her, but, after all, they were only boys ; he had not Uncle Robert's fatherly ways, nor their crudeness. Perhaps Ada's vanity had been touched by the attentions.

A spasm of the old jealous feeling stole over her. She did not love to share whatever was hers with any other person, and that Emma should show her gladness at his coming, that he should appear so pleased with her wordless recognition — But what if — their friendship was older, certainly, and it might

12

be something deeper than friendship. Ada had been
quick to spy out the meaning of such things.

Then she suddenly checked her surmises, and put
aside her pained, exacting self. Why should not Mr.
Langdon care for Emma ? and why should she thrust
away the simple pleasures of friendship because another had something sweeter and finer ?

So the cloudy brow cleared up, and the perplexity
seemed to roll away like a summer mist. Strange,
too, she felt better after the effort had been made, and
she resolved as well not to whisper her suspicion to
Kathie, to take pattern by the child's delicacy and
reticence.

They had a lovely drive, and found a group gathered at the wide-open hall door to welcome them.
Farmer Strong and his sons had made a little improvement at the front this spring. There was a new
fence and a neat gate, and two clumps of evergreens
beautified the old-fashioned door-yard. Then the
stone steps had been relaid, and the whole place
wore an improved air.

Mr. and Mrs. Strong were profuse in their welcome.
Indeed, they esteemed the visit of any friend of Kathie as quite a compliment. Ada took off her hat

and sack in the best room, gave a glance at herself in the old-fashioned glass, and then they were all marshalled out to supper.

The table literally groaned with good things. To be sure, the China was in the most glaring of colors, and the forks steel, with only two tines; but the cloth was snowy white and thick as velvet, and napkins, and the most generous hospitality. The "children" were ranged down one side, with Cousin Ellen to look after them, and Ada admitted that they behaved very well, if they were rather free with their English.

"Your friend does n't look very rugged, Miss Kathie. City girls are 'most always pale and thin. They stay in the house, sit up late nights, and lace too much, and then never have any appetite. Why, child, you don't eat enough to keep a mouse alive!"

Ada blushed and smiled, yet appeared a little dismayed at the quantity on her plate, that she had taken to please Mrs. Strong. Kathie explained that her friend had been an invalid for some time.

"There is nothing in the world like good country air and wholesome food," declared the farmer, "and then not *too* much study. Gals get worn out before they are women nowadays."

Sarah colored warmly. She did not want her
father to air his pet hobby before Kathie's stylish
friend, and changed the conversation with a grace
that one would hardly have expected. Uncle Robert
understood it and assisted, meeting Sarah's quick,
grateful glance. How much tact, and what a fine
sense the girl was developing!

Presently the strangeness wore off, and they were
all exceedingly cordial. Even Ada seemed to catch
the infection, and laid aside her sense of dignity, forgot the obtrusive self that usually haunted her.

They had the loveliest of moonlight to ride home
in, though the Strongs would fain have kept them
later in the evening.

Kathie leaned back in her seat and gave a half-
sigh.

" Are you tired?" asked her uncle.

" Pleasantly tired "; and she smiled a little. " I
had to go all over the farm to see every new tree and
shrub, and the horses and cows and chickens, and
— everything. We have talked steadily, I believe,
and I feel as if I had been 'out visiting.' It was
very good of you to come, Ada, and gives you a little
glimpse of real country. I hope you were not wea-
ried."

" On the contrary, I was a good deal interested. But how *do* they manage with so many children ? "

" I suppose it does n't seem a great many to them. And how nice it will be when they are grown up and married, and come home to Thanksgiving dinners ! I wish we had a dozen children."

Ada thought how often she had wished herself an only child, and how, since the reverse of fortune, she had almost grudged the money spent upon the others. Ah, how narrow and selfish her soul really was !

" How generous it was of you to take so much pains with that Sarah Strong ! " Ada said, as they were preparing for bed. " But I should be afraid that people of that stamp would — presume."

" If there is anything nice, and any lifting up in this world, why should n't they get their share ? And I often think they have more real, true delicacy than many of whom you might rightfully expect it."

" That was going out of the way to find work, I am sure," Ada said, with a half-smile, rather doubtful, as if she was not fully satisfied.

" Was it ? No, I think it came right in my way. And it seemed to be one of the very ' least of these.'

Ever since all the good and enchanting fortune came to me I have been trying to give thanks, not in words only, but in making other lives a little bit pleasanter, if I could; and I feel as if it was the poor and barren ways that wanted to be taught to blossom, not those with roses already in them."

A great choking seemed to rise in Ada's throat. Something had been in her heart for many days, at times vexing her through very perverseness, and then rendering her grateful in spite of herself.

"I heard," she began, in a low tone, averting her face, "that you might have gone to the White Mountains with a pleasant party. You gave it up in order to — "

"Not altogether," exclaimed Kathie, with a quick flush and a little quiver through all her pulses. Mamma could not go, nor Emma, and I would rather have stayed at home anyhow. But I am very glad if — "

"It has been a pleasant visit, and I have improved in health, perhaps in some other ways as well. You were very kind to think of it, to do it. Good night."

Ada's voice was husky, and she turned abruptly away. Kathie did not feel slighted because there was no warmer demonstration. She understood that it would be very hard for Ada, after always having held herself loftily above her, to confess herself in any secondary position. And Kathie had learned the grandest and sweetest part of Divine charity, not to seek her own. It was enough that the work was done. So long as the sheaves came in, it made little difference whether they were laid at her feet or not.

"The boys are on their homeward route," said Uncle Robert one morning. "Rob is in despair because vacation is so nearly over."

Mrs. Alston smiled. Rob would be himself only to the end of boyhood, or even life.

Ada had letters too. A brief, rather fault-finding, note from her mother, and quite a lengthy letter from her father. He had been spending several days at the seaside, but from the tone of his reference to it Ada judged that it had not been much of a rest or refreshment. He seemed, indeed, weary and discouraged. Their cook was discharged, and the house shut up. Edward had insisted upon his brother's sharing his home comforts, which he had been very glad to do. Was it the difference in love and devotion and tenderness that so moved him?

Ada's eyes had been opened to many things. Heretofore it seemed as if she and her mother had been
the greatest sufferers by their reverses. Had not her
father lost incalculably as well? In past times his
home had proved bright and elegant, made so by an
abundance of money and choice serving, rather than
that any one had studied his comfort. Now there
were toilsome, perplexing days, but who ever tried to
brighten the evenings? Her mother was full of the
worry of servants and the many privations she had to
endure, or, if there were no guests in, often spent
the evening on the sofa with a headache. He was
trying to make it better for them all, — but was it
not their duty to do something in return?

According to Aunt Ruth, the boys had enjoyed
themselves royally, and been no trouble to anybody.
They had fished and hunted, explored rivers and
mountains and the camps of friendly Indians, been
lost two or three times, and had several hair-breadth
escapes. And, above all, she confessed to Kathie that
Bruce was the tenderest and manliest of sons.

The days flew by so rapidly that, before one was
really expecting it, a telegram came from New York,
announcing that a whole party were on their way to

Brookside, the two others being Jessie and Mr. Meredith. So they made ready to welcome them, and went over to the station in the great family carriage.

Somebody gave a shout as the train stopped. Rob, of course. There he was, so brown you could hardly see the roses on his cheeks, and with his curly hair cropped close ; but nothing could ever take the laughing twinkle out of his eyes.

" Is n't it jolly ? O Kathie, how white you are, — a regular pale-face ! Dear Uncle Rob ! How is mother, and Fred, and everybody ? O Ada !" Rob stopped there and blushed, and Bruce came up to share the honors of the occasion.

Kathie really felt shy of him, — a veritable young man, taller than Uncle Robert, and with a soft dark mustache, as dainty as if it had grown according to order. Ada received him in her graceful, ladylike way, but Kathie scarcely spoke at all, and blushed every time the dark eyes were turned upon her.

" How are you, Meredith ? " and Uncle Robert grasped his hand warmly. " You and Jessie ride over with us, and we will send you home afterward. We must plead guilty to a little selfishness, for we did not share our telegram, consequently Mr Darrell will not know the exact time of your arrival."

"We shall have to look out for you in future returned Jessie, laughingly. "We wanted to be su that these young travellers reached their friends in safety, lest they might be tempted to turn back to their wild life."

"Thank you."

"There never was anything quite so splendid!" Rob was going on rapturously. "To think of actually hunting buffaloes and being out in one Indian skirmish! Aunt Ruth would n't let me write home about it, for fear mother would be frightened. They were on a thieving raid, and stole some horses, and part of the garrison went out from the fort. Two of the Indians were killed, and one of our men wounded."

"Rob had a mind to enlist in the regular army," said Bruce.

"It is great fun."

"For a summer vacation," replied Mr. Meredith. "If you had only brought Aunt Ruth home!"

"What would my father have done?" and then

Bruce blushed, while the rest laughed at his out-spoken honesty.

"Dear me, how little and crowded everything looks!" declared Rob. "It almost stifles you to get back to civilization again. And how are all the boys?"

Kathie was expected to keep the run of the boys, and all other matters that appeared of importance to Rob. So she gave a very clear statement.

By this time they were home, and had the warmest of welcomes from mamma. Jessie and Mr. Meredith must certainly stay to supper, so they went up stairs to wash the dust of travel off of their faces.

"Ada, you look like a new being," said Jessie. "How delighted Dr. Markham will be! And your papa sent ever so many loving messages. We almost persuaded him to come, but it was difficult for both to leave. He wished that he might answer your last letter in person."

The tears made a quick rush to Ada's eyes, but she would not let them drop. Did he like it then, that tiny glimpse of her heart and some of the new purposes of her life? O, if she could have strength and grace to realize any of them!

"Yes, Kathie has surely been feeding you on the elixir of health and roses," said her uncle, putting his arm around her, and going back to the old fancy he had for her as a child. "I wonder that Dr. Markham can approve of her at all, since she interferes with the regular business. It is opposition to imposition. I expect she will be studying medicine next, and setting up for a physician."

"I think I will take patients when they are almost well, and have the credit," she returned, gayly.

They went down stairs to supper, a merry crowd indeed, and before they were through Mr. Langdon came over to see what had happened, while Dick heard at the station, and made a rush straightway. Rob would certainly be the hero of the evening.

Ada took a fancy to ride over with her aunt and uncle, and the rest disposed themselves on the piazza steps to discuss Western life. But presently Bruce begged Kathie to take a turn through the walks with him. "For I have so much to say — about *her*. O Kathie, you don't know what it is to have been hungry all your life for a little mother-love, to see other boys going home to mothers and sisters, and understand that there was none for you. But it has come now."

"I am so glad." She felt more than ever willing to give up her dear Aunt Ruth.

"When she came to West Point we had only time for the merest visit and talk, and it was so strange to think of her being father's wife, and sort of taking my place in his heart, and he being so occupied and satisfied with her, I was afraid it would be more lonesome than ever for me, and that I would not have the first right to anybody."

"Oh!" Kathie exclaimed, with a touch of sudden pain. "I suppose that is where it seems so hard to have a step-mother."

"If I had had one when I was a little chap — but my father has loved me alone for years and years. And I was some jealous, I guess. You see, I am confessing all my badness to you, Kathie, for you and she are so much alike. I told her all about it afterward. I am so glad we went out, Rob and I. We were a bit strange at first. Father said long ago that he would not insist upon my calling her mother, but if I could cheerfully it would be a great pleasure to him. So I always did. What are you smiling about? — for I know you are, though I can hardly see it."

"The idea of Aunt Ruth having such a big son. Please don't be vexed," the soft voice entreated.

"I could not be vexed with you anyway. Well, it was one thing to write it in letters, but quite another to say it. I think she understood my awkwardness, and perhaps the other little feeling, for the very first evening we were alone she told me she wanted a good long talk, and we had it — just splendid. After it was all through I don't believe I could have loved an own mother any better. She explained it all to me so beautifully, — that there was room enough in my father's heart for both of us, and that I must love him just as well as I did before, and never let any distrust creep in between us. By degrees, she said, I would learn to love and trust her. As if I could help doing it there on the spot! And then, you know, we were the very best of friends, and have had the sweetest time, — is n't that what you girls say? I believe I have never been so happy in my whole life. I could not bear to come away, any more than Rob."

"I am so thankful to have you love her as she deserves."

"It would be shameful if I did not, when she has been so good. I only wonder how you could bear to give her up."

" I had mamma and Uncle Robert, you know, but I did feel very lonesome at first. Only I guess I was not consulted about it," she continued, archly.

" I suppose they did not need either of us in council beforehand," Bruce said, laughingly. " And I am so glad that father is very happy. He is so thoroughly good and noble. It is strange that he should have taken such a great fancy to you at the first."

Kathie remembered. A simple, eager, happy country child she was then. And, going farther back, was it not Aunt Ruth who had helped her to correct her faults, and strive for the higher graces ?

It seemed so odd just then that she had to tell Bruce about the giants, and they had a good laugh.

" I believe I shall have to go to work and hunt some up, for the rascals lurk around always. It is such a great thing to have some one help you a little in the warfare."

It was indeed. Kathie felt how much she owed, and the only way to pay was to assist others.

" This is my last year at West Point. And you

cannot guess, Kathie, what is coming afterward. O, I forgot"; and he checked himself.

"A happy home maybe."

He drew her hand through his arm, and held the small fingers in an eager, boyish fashion, as if his secret was indeed hard to keep.

"I promised not to tell, so I must not say a word, only I *do* wish it was next June. You must not betray me by admitting to any one that I roused your curiosity."

Kathie laughed musically, not guessing that the secret in any way concerned her.

"'Upon my word and honor,'" she replied. "Will that do? And now, when do Aunt Ruth and your father intend to return?"

"I don't know. There are always so many halts in government business. Still, he wants to be back before cold weather. After this year he means to retire from the army. But mother has enjoyed the Western trip very much. I believe she grows prettier and rosier all the time. And I am very glad that she likes boys."

Kathie laughed over that. If she could be sweet and patient with such a boisterous fellow as Rob, surely she might be tender to Bruce.

They walked up and down under the trees until all the strangeness wore off. Once, when she spoke of his father, he said, "Why don't you call him uncle? I like to feel that he is something to you as well. And I am going to claim my right of cousinship in every particular."

"I have never had any cousins that I remember," she answered, slowly.

Rob was equally enthusiastic about Aunt Ruth. "She is something of a stunner, after all," he declared in his impulsive way. "You ought to see the deference the men pay to her, quite as if she were a queen. They would any of them go ten miles to serve her. I often think of the time I knocked down Lu Simonds for his impudence about her. Our poor dear crippled Aunt Ruth! It is like a fairy story to think of her getting well and marrying such a great man."

"And very delightful, I am sure."

Bruce had just four days to stay at Cedarwood. He made so many cousinly demands upon Kathie that she was afraid Ada would feel herself slighted. Rob went half crazy over the boys, as if, when he was once swallowed up inside of college walls, he would

13

never see them again. There was a continual going and coming, and Hannah declared that any other woman beside Mrs. Alston would lose her senses.

Then there was a sudden scattering of the forces. Bruce said a last lingering good-by one morning, after making Kathie promise a dozen times over to write, and then Mr. and Mrs. Meredith took their departure, Jessie extorting a promise from Kathie that she would be sure to spend Christmas with them.

Then began some more important preparations. Rob's college outfit was nearly ready. His uncle was to go with him to New Haven, stopping over one night in New York and making some purchases.

" I am thankful that he will have Dick Grayson's companionship," Mrs. Alston said. " It seems to me that he is wilder and more impetuous than ever. I do not know as the Western trip was the best thing for him, after all. I thought he was getting quite calmed down."

" He is a healthy, irrepressible boy, and we shall be able to make nothing else of him for some years to come; but he does grow in wisdom and moral strength. Dick's influence will tend to preserve the balance, I hope."

Rob, Dick, Fred, and Charlie had some royal good rambles and rowing-matches. Fred had pretty nearly recovered his strength, but the doctor declared that it would not do for him to work as hard another year.

"He *is* real heroic," declared Rob. "Here we lazy fellows think it a great thing if we study when all the rest is done for us, but he works and studies both. Now if he could have an uncle and a fortune drop from the clouds as ours did !"

"Oh!" exclaimed Kathie. "I give thanks for it every day of my life. It has brought us so much happiness."

CHAPTER XI.

FROM PLEASURE TO WORK.

"GOOD by ! Good by !"

With that Rob was off again. Mrs. Alston wiped away a few tears. It seemed as if she had so little of her boy nowadays. Here was Freddy, to be sure, sweet and loving, and not half the trouble of head-strong, wayward Rob. And yet, how her heart went out to him continually! He always thought of her when he said his prayers night and morning, if at no other time ; but she carried him in her heart always.

Kathie and Ada waved a last adieu. The house seemed very quiet now that the raiders had all dispersed. Indeed, they hardly knew what to do after so much excitement.

"I shall have to be thinking about school myself," Kathie said. "This lovely, lazy life has been enchanting."

Ada made no reply. What was she to think about ? The season was still exceedingly warm, and

Mrs. Meredith did not propose to return until it was cooler. Uncle Edward had asked her to come and spend a week or two with them, but Mr. Conover had insisted that she should stay and have the utmost benefit of the healthful country air. But would it not be pleasant for her father's sake ?

Would she have the courage to take up the duties that lay so clearly in her path, — to be an earnest, helpful daughter, a patient sister ? She had many old longings for society, admiration, and pretty dressing, but none of these would come much in her way for the present. Should she refuse the things she might have, — the simple, inexpensive pleasures, the opportunity of making others happy, — and sink back into her olden sloth and apathy ?

She was beginning to understand, slowly and faintly, like one long blind, that however much the kingdom of this world might be from without, the kingdom of heaven was within the soul's province ; and this it was that added the grand satisfaction to life. But it was a strait and narrow path. Could she walk in it ?

Mr. Langdon dropped in a little while at twilight. " Brookside will be inconsolable," he said. " It is about as bad as the war-times when every one went marching off. Fred goes in a day or two ; and Emma wanted me to ask you to come over to tea to-morrow night. Fred thinks they have done all the visiting."

" With pleasure," returned Kathie. " Our time for dissipation is nearly ended. It has been a delightful summer."

" A very happy one — to me."

There was something peculiar in Mr. Langdon's voice. Kathie had never heard it there before, she thought.

" I am glad," she said, earnestly. " There is n't anything quite like happiness in this world, — at least, not so sweet."

" No. And you have not guessed what event has given me mine ? "

They were out on the porch alone. Kathie raised her puzzled face, and a rift of color crossed his. And then something came into her mind. A few days ago Rob had said, " Mr. Langdon is pretty sweet on Emma Lauriston, is n't he ? " Was it anything —

" Emma wanted you to know, but she had not the courage to tell. It is not to be a long engagement, so we do not care to keep our secret. I can't help thinking that she is ever so much like you, and I believe that was what attracted me first."

" Oh!" Kathie exclaimed, in the utmost humility.

" Yes. She told me all about the old school troubles, and how you first came to be such dear friends."

" She was very brave and noble," Kathie rejoined, quickly.

" And we thought it a little ungrateful not to ask you in to our feast," he said, with a smile. " Are you not going to wish me all sorts of pleasant things? though I suppose it is quite impossible for you to take as much interest in us as in the Merediths."

" I am sure you have been very kind to Rob, to us all. And I know you will be happy, so I wish you — everything."

" Thank you. Did n't you really suspect? O you innocent little girl! I dare say your friend guessed it. Come over to-morrow, or Fred will feel that you have exhausted your sympathy over the other boys, and have none left for him."

Kathie went up to the sitting-room thoughtfully Ada was on Aunt Ruth's crimson lounge reading, so she gave her the invitation.

"And Mr. Langdon and Emma are — "

"Engaged !" Ada laughed a little. "It has grown
rather transparent of late, so I supposed it would come
out soon. It seems to me there has been a great deal
of falling in love in this house."

Kathie sat down by the open window to think. It
seemed so strange. Yes, there had been Jessie and
Mr. Meredith, Aunt Ruth and General Mackenzie :
but she could make them grown-up people in her
mind, while Emma was almost like herself; and she
felt awed with the mystery.

"She ought to be a very happy girl," Ada said
presently, with a half-sigh, remembering her own
foolishly ambitious dreams. "Mr. Langdon is a
gentleman."

"And good and noble and generous."

They had a quiet, pleasant visit, but the atmosphere seemed to have something odd in it. Emma
blushed if any one looked at her, and her voice was
full of tremulous breaks. She and Kathie never said
a word about the secret, but there was a very tender
sympathy between them.

"I never saw anything like it in my life," Sue
Coleman said, a week afterward, on her return

" Here we girls went off husband-hunting, and dispensed our sweetest smiles around, while Emma stayed at home and captured the hero. Why, I was keeping an eye on him myself! I think he is fully as nice as your Mr. Meredith."

Ada had proposed to her father that she should return home and get the house in a little order before her mother returned, and he gladly acceded. Jessie had heard of a neat woman who was willing to come and do the cleaning.

" It shows that Ada has improved," Mrs. Alston said, much gratified. " Your summer's work has not all been in vain."

" Everybody has helped me continually. And, mamma, I think I am beginning to love Ada truly."

" She is showing herself more worthy of love. I used to feel a little afraid of her influence over you, lest you might fall into her foolish habits and beliefs."

They had never been very inviting to a girl like Kathie, and the sweet home influence had possessed her soul from the first.

Ada was very sorry to go, even after she had resolved. " It will be so much harder for me at home," she said to Mrs. Alston. " Our habits of life and thought are so different. I shall have no one to help me in my many discouragements."

" There is One who never fails, never forgets. You must call upon him for strength, my dear child. He will answer to the uttermost."

" If I could believe, could only trust. But it seems as if God could not care very much for one, when there are so many in the world needing his pity and help."

" Yet if he cares for the flowers of the field and the birds of the air, will he so easily forget us ? Only try him, Ada."

" I dare say I shall wish myself back hundreds of times," she confessed to Kathie. " I don't wonder that everybody gets to loving Cedarwood."

" And when you are tired out you can come back for a week or two to rest. Even if I am in school we shall have some time to visit."

" I shall want to come often."

It was a really sad parting at the last, and the house seemed very lonesome when they were all gone. But school began the next week.

None of the older girls came back. To make

amends there were some new ones who were old
friends of Kathie, — Mary Cox and several others.
"But much of the charm is gone out of it," she told
Uncle Robert.

"All the duty is left, I suppose?" and there was a
half-mirthful, half-grave twinkle in his eye.

Rob confessed to being homesick the first fortnight.
The course of study was hard, half of the fellows were
prigs, and the "Sophs" he hated. He was not sure
but that he would rather go into some kind of business, or out on the frontier.

"He will soon get interested. It is only the natural reaction."

"I can understand it, for I feel a little so myself,"
Kathie said, with a smile.

Ada, meanwhile, had more than satisfied her father
with her improvement. He was looking thin and
worn, and showing his age. She had never realized
how much she might be to him as when he took her
in his arms and kissed her with a sad tenderness.
Ah, there had a great deal gone out of his life!

The woman made her appearance in a day or two,
— a strong, good-hearted German, willing to undertake anything. So they went over to the deserted

house, let in the sunshine, and set about making the rooms presentable.

After her chamber had a thorough sweeping and airing, Ada determined to put it in order herself. There was a good deal of work in going over closets and drawers, and clearing out useless garments, faded finery, and half-worn shoes. How had so much rubbish collected?

"I am sure I don't know what to do with it," she said, hopelessly.

"O Miss Meredith, if there is anything you don't want, give it to me! My sister is a widow, and has five children to clothe, so any trifle comes in good."

Here was a deed of kindness right in the way. It did not seem as if those old, soiled, rumpled garments could be of any service, but the widow with five children must be much poorer than she. And somehow her heart warmed with the thought of benefiting the needy, — a new feeling for her.

The day was almost gone when she finished her room. It seemed a very little work to spend so much time over, yet she felt tired enough to stop. Christine had gone through her father's room and the nursery, putting the latter in complete order.

"You may as well take the broken toys, if you care for them," she said, glancing at the miscellaneous pile.

"O thank you, thank you!"

"What a grateful creature!" she thought.

Christine found a large basket, and packed them in. She would take the key, as she meant to come bright and early the next morning. Ada had smoothed her hair and changed her dress, and now bade the woman good by with thoughtful courtesy.

Jessie was becoming rather worried about her, and welcomed her with a cordial kiss, putting her in the great easy-chair, and not allowing her to stir until the gentlemen came home.

"Be a little careful, and do not wear yourself out," was Jessie's sage advice the next morning.

"O, I don't do any of the real hard work. Christine is so willing and ready. If we could only get a servant like her!"

"I do believe a pleasant mistress usually makes cheerful servants. They are human beings like ourselves, and can feel hurt with sharp words or cross looks."

Ada smiled a little. "I am afraid if Mary had

wasted all day arranging my room and closets I should have found fault. I know mamma would. And yet I worked faithfully myself."

"I dare say. The trouble is, until we do some of these things for ourselves, we do not realize how much time they take. We may sometimes scold a servant when she has been very faithful, and perhaps her only way of retaliating is next time to be careless. We all need more wisdom and patience to make the race of mistresses perfect," Jessie said, with her bright look.

Ada went at her work with renewed energy. Her mother's belongings she did not touch, but her father's clothes were brushed and put in order, the soiled ones being laid aside for the wash. The sitting-room needed very little overlooking, so they came to the parlors. Christine swept first, and while she washed paint and windows, Ada dusted. If they could only get through with that before night!

"Here is a carriage at the door," exclaimed Christine, "and — an old gentleman."

Ada's face was scarlet. She thought in a moment of her tumbled hair and her disordered dress. She had just taken the music out of the rack and scattered it over the floor, and hoped sincerely it was no one to see her. Then she caught the voice, — Dr. Markham's.

"Hey! hey!" he exclaimed, marching in. "This is a good thing for weak eyes, — such a sight! Why, child, you are as rosy as a peony, and improved — forty per cent! I would not have believed it! And actually making yourself useful!"

Ada could have cried with a sense of mortification, and the apparent ridiculousness of the whole scene. But he strode over and seemed to pick her out of the ruins, and kissed her, a thing he had not done for years.

"My child," he said, with deep feeling, "God knows how glad I am to find you improved in soul and body. I have been very anxious for your welfare, and when I heard from Mrs. Edward to-day, I could not resist dropping in. You had a pleasant time, and were neither bored nor homesick?"

"Very pleasant." Her voice quivered a little.

"I hope it may be the beginning of a new life. You are so young that you can make it almost what you will. There is something better than vanity and frivolity. If our girls would only learn the truth, we might hope for a better race of women."

Ada did not reply. Her knowledge was so new and uncertain, and she was learning that the deep undercurrents of feeling could not so easily be put into words.

"I guess you have done enough for one day. The air is very fine, so you had better put on some of your fixings and take a drive with me. I want to hear all about Cedarwood, like any other old gossip."

"But I am in such a plight," Ada said, deprecatingly.

"O, you can remedy that in a few moments."

"And I ought not to leave my work unfinished"; with a smile. "You will lead me back into bad habits again."

"Nonsense! Run and get ready."

Ada went up stairs and sat down on the edge of her bed in despair. In ten minutes Dr. Markham's patience would be exhausted. What could she do? There was her hair to arrange, her dress to change, and a little dust surely must be washed off. O dear!

But she went at it in good earnest. No elaborate puffs and braids this time. She combed her hair, gave it a loose twist, and slipped a net over it; and somehow everything went smoothly, so that she did not much exceed the ten minutes. But it was a very simple toilet, yet it was seldom indeed that she looked prettier.

"You deserve a bright penny, latest issue, and I am sorry I have n't one. What is to be done with this woman ? — for I doubt if I bring you back here. Can she shut up shop herself?"

"O yes." Then she gave Christine a few directions, and, nodding gayly, went out.

"Kathie will need to look well to her laurels, I think. It would be barbarous for an old man like me to prove inconstant at the eleventh hour, but you have grown quite captivating, Miss Ada. I begin to have some misgivings."

"O, you need not," she replied, laughingly, meeting the droll twinkle in his eye that always betrayed an unusually genial mood.

"And now tell me what sort of a time you have had. Are the headaches gone, and can you sleep well ? Have you taken any walks, and how is the weakness in your limbs, and the fluttering pulses ?"

"I believe I am thoroughly well."

"A blessing to be most thankful for. Don't fritter it away again, but live as a reasonable human being

14

should, who was sent into the world for some use a
trifle above the sloth or the butterfly, though I dare
say they serve their purpose better than many of us.
How do you like real good honest earnest living ? "

Ada turned a blushing and perplexed face towards
him.

" I jumble my questions together too much, do I ?
Well, we will take them a little more moderately.
Cedarwood was better than the seaside ? "

" I think it was."

" You wanted companionship of the right kind, and
a chance to use your faculties. Too many people in
this world get rusty and decrepit and helpless before
they have found out what they can do. If it is true
that we go to Skitzland when we die, and that whatever powers we fail to use here are taken from us
there, what a set of cripples we shall be, both mentally and physically ! "

" That is a new world," returned Ada, in amusement.

" Belonging to an old philosopher. He paid it a
visit one day, and found people who could not walk,
others who had lost the cunning of their right hand
or their left, or the faculties of their mind and soul,

— a set of grinning, chattering idiots, I dare say. It behooves us to be careful, for fear it *might* be the intermediate sphere "; and his grim lips relaxed mirthfully.

" What of the boys ? " he asked, after a few moments' silence.

So Ada detailed snatches of her visit. She had improved a good deal in health, and perhaps not a little in wisdom. The old troublesome self was not as obtrusive as formerly. She had been roused to take an interest in the things about her. Dr. Markham rubbed his hands mentally, and gave Kathie bits of quiet praise just under his breath.

One of the greatest improvements was that she had become capable of appreciating the Doctor's sterling good sense, even if he was a little brusque. She felt attracted to him as she never had been before, and when she realized her own weakness, she understood the necessity of drawing about her the strong, kind friends who would not disdain to aid in an emergency.

By Friday Ada and Christine had the house in complete order, and it happened very fortunately, for Mr. Meredith brought home a letter from his wife, desiring him to come down and bring Ada, as she had made arrangements to return the first of the following week.

"Then we shall begin in earnest," the young girl thought. "Heaven give me grace and strength to try!"

CHAPTER XII.

EXPERIENCE WORKETH HOPE.

"THE loveliest of all letters!" Kathie exclaimed, rapturously. "Three, mamma, only think! Aunt Ruth expects to be home at Christmas, and will spend all the spring with us. Is n't that royal? And Jessie Meredith has the sweetest little boy in the world, and his name is — Can you guess what?"

Mrs. Alston smiled.

"O, you have heard too!"

"Uncle Robert had a note from Mr. Meredith."

"And the baby is to be Robert Conover Meredith. They will have to call him Robin for short, and to distinguish him from the others of the same name, for fear he will get mixed up. Jessie's baby! Is n't it odd? I want to see it so much that I can hardly wait."

"And your other letter?"

"Is from Ada. Mamma, I do believe she is trying to do her very best. I wish there were more bright and encouraging things in her life, or if she had a mother like mine."

Kathie's arms were around her mother's neck, and the warm, eager lips pressed closely against the others, so dear.

" Thank you, my darling."

The child laughed with a sweet, dainty ring.

" For wishing other people were like you? Is it so much of a compliment? But Ada likes you a great deal."

"And it is pleasant to be considered lovable."

Kathie gave her another tender kiss.

" And we have heard from Rob," said her mother, " so it may be considered a day of letters."

" O, how is he?"

" Well, and getting somewhat accustomed to the routine of study. Indeed, he writes in very good spirits."

"There is Uncle Robert"; and she was off like a bird.

The new namesake was a marvel. Uncle Robert had been asked to come down to the christening.

" I will have to endow it with half of my fortune, — how will that do?" he asked, laughingly.

"No, he can have but a quarter," she answered, in a merry tone.

"But you have been invited as well. Now, if he takes a slice of yours — "

"We will endow him with love instead. O, can I really go? When is it to be?"

"In a fortnight, on Tuesday, so it will keep you out of school half a week; but as you had no summer excursion, we will be indulgent."

"But I have something all the time. Uncle Robert, did you ever think what a delightful thing it is to live and to be so happy, just like a bird? Why, I am brimful!"

He looked at the glad little face dimpled with smiles and tinted by roses. One always had a reward in bestowing favors or pleasures upon her, she was so glad and enjoyed them so thoroughly. And the thing that came was always the best, no matter what might have been in its stead.

Then she had to tell about Aunt Ruth. "It will seem just like old times to have her back again, and to stay for months. It hardly seems true."

She danced along by his side in the mellow orange tint of the October sunshine, verging into Indian

summer, — a bright, winsome child in many moods,
as now, and then shady, thoughtful touches of the
coming woman.

At school she was studying hard, intent upon graduating another year. Her mother managed now that
the duties outside should be more of pleasure and
interest than actual work. There were numerous
pets and *protégés* in the village, and friends who
shared her love, but the same judicious hand carefully weeded them out, that the claims should not be
too onerous. For Kathie's years and station would
have given her quite a position, had her mother so
willed.

" I do not wish her to be a woman too soon," she
would say. " Every new sphere brings with it fresh
claims and cares."

Kathie and Emma had many shy, sweet confidences.
Reticent by nature, and having no nearer relative
than her grandmother, Emma had lived much from
within, making a world for herself, until she had
known the Alstons. Some of the truest and tenderest graces had come fresh from Kathie, and it always
gave her a thrill of humility when her lover said,
playfully, of any little speech, " That is a decided
Kathie-ism."

Mrs. Adams had taken up the young girl in a kind
of grave, elder-sister fashion that awed her a trifle.
They were to be married about the holidays, and
spend the intervening time until spring with his sister. Fortunately a second or third cousin had come
to visit Grandmother Lauriston, and decided to make
it her home in future. She was a widow of about
fifty and possessed of some means.

"I believe everything always does happen just
right," Emma said to Kathie. "I was troubled about
leaving grandmother alone, but Cousin Esther is such
a nice, sweet, quiet body that I shall not have a single
care. And Mr. Langdon is so generous. After I am
married, he wants me to let Fred have my income to
help him along for the next two years, so that he will
not have to work so hard. And I am to go on with
painting, though I shall never enter the School of
Design now. How strange it all seems!"

Then there were pretty, dainty garments to be
made, and Cousin Esther came in handy again.
Emma's slender fingers were always busy, since she
chose to do most of these things for herself. Kathie
undertook a small gift of needlework, — to fill up her
spare moments, she said, though they were quite rare

at this juncture. But her heart's love went into every stitch and every flower.

She was doubly grateful for the opportunity of visiting New York, as she did want to see Ada. She went to school on Friday morning for her recitations only, and at noon they started on their journey.

Jessie was most glad to see them. They found her in the loveliest of blue cashmere wrappers, looking indescribably sweet, if a little less rosy than usual. Master Robin had been promoted to a pretty crib and dainty white blankets, and was so soundly asleep that the talking did not wake him. He had a broad white forehead and an abundance of black hair, which his fond mother brushed into a curl on the top of his head.

"And the most beautiful eyes, Kathie, for all the world like a purple pansy. Edward thinks they will come out blue, and I am sure they will be dark like his. It is so odd to have a baby of one's very own, and quite laughable to imagine that ridiculous mite growing into a man."

"Why, I don't see that he looks at all ridiculous," Kathie answered, gravely. It seemed to her that he was wonderfully pretty, with his rosebud of a mouth,

and ears that were like a delicate shell, to say nothing of the dimpled fists, doubled up as if he held a
fortune inside of them.

Mrs. Darrell came in to welcome Kathie. They
had waited supper for the travellers, and now all was
ready. Jessie decided not to go down, as she had
been about considerably during the day, but begged
them not to hurry on her account.

Mr. Meredith declared he was dying to have Kathie's opinion of the baby. Was it not the smartest
and most beautiful baby she had ever seen?

"I do not feel competent to judge of its abilities
on so short an acquaintance," she answered, with
mock seriousness. "He certainly looks pretty."

"You will have a proof of his ability before this
time to-morrow," Mr. Meredith returned, laughingly.
"He is a noisy little youngster when he starts about
it. I have my suspicions that he means to pattern
after Robert the second."

"I am afraid we all had a touch of the complaint,"
said Uncle Robert.

"Noise and boys and Fourth of July and fireworks
are connected together by an indestructible chain."

"I am sure he is a very good baby," said Mrs. Darrell, rather resenting the inference. " He would not know much if he did not know how to cry."

" Now really ! " was Mr. Meredith's quizzical rejoinder. " Well, we will give him the credit of being amiable by spells. I think it would be a good plan to keep Kathie here for nurse."

Kathie smiled. The two gentlemen lingered over their dessert, as they had fallen into a business talk, and, begging to be excused, she ran up stairs to Jessie. The baby was up now, staring at the light with a wide intentness in his eyes, as if he was determined to fathom the mystery.

" O, can't I hold him a little while ? " Kathie exclaimed, and Jessie put him in her arms.

He studied her then in his deliberate baby fashion, and gave a soft, gurgling sound that was inexpressibly sweet.

" He is a darling ! " said Kathie, delightedly.

Mr. Meredith asked her. when he came up, if she had already engaged, what her wages were, and how many days " out " she must have. Baby seemed to have forgotten his worrying spell, for he sat quiet in her lap, soothed by the caressing voice, until his eyelids began to droop.

"He is on his very best behavior," declared his father. "You see he does not wish to frighten you in the beginning."

Jessie laid him in the crib presently, and then she took Kathie to her room to show her all his pretty clothes.

"Ada sent me this little skirt. She embroidered it herself. You know she has never done any kind of sewing, so I thought it was very sweet in her to take so much trouble. She is counting on your visit, and I suppose I shall have to give you up to-morrow."

"She has the courage to go on then?"

"Yes, and it does take a good deal, Kathie. If her mother could but understand and help her! She has much encouragement from her father, and I believe she succeeds in making his home more pleasant and inviting. Her mother has begun to go into society again, and really urges Ada into dissipation. I tremble for the good seed sown with so many prayers."

"O, I hope Ada will be strong!"

"I think her soul might be cultured to something finer than these paltry shows and aims. Mrs. Meredith would be much mortified if Ada did not marry within a year or two, and she is trying to win her back to the old creed. It provokes Dr. Markham so much. He has taken a wonderful interest in Ada."

"Dear Dr. Markham!" Kathie said, with girlish fondness. "He is so good to all out-of-the-way suffering and weakness."

"That is just it. The ordinary, thrusting itself out to every one's notice, he passes by. There are enough to minister to such cases, and I believe he has a dislike to evils that glory in parading themselves; at least, he is always sharp and impatient with them."

"I can never forget how tender he was to Aunt Ruth. I did feel a good deal afraid of him at first," she confessed, with an arch smile.

"You two inveterate gossips!" exclaimed Mr. Meredith. "Come back and help entertain us. Why are girls and women forever lingering in corners and nooks and talking over secrets?"

"As if we could not have some business of our own!" Kathie returned, saucily.

He pinched the peachy cheek. "Sit down here and tell me everything about Cedarwood. Mr. Langdon, I hear, has been snared, taken captive. I begin to think it a dangerous place"; and he shook his head gravely.

"O yes," rejoined Jessie, "mother was speaking
of it. Emma Lauriston is a lovely girl, and I am glad
she is going to do so well, though I did not suspect
him a bit."

"And what else has happened?"

Nothing of importance, it seemed, yet they had a
pleasant chat before they separated for the night.

Dr. Markham was in early the next morning, and
invited Kathie to tea on Monday evening. Then, as
she was ready, he offered to take her to Ada's.

"My dear child," he said, when he had settled her
beside him, "I want to thank you for your pains and
trouble of last summer, and the self-denial too. I
heard about your invitation to the White Mountains."

"O," Kathie said, deprecatingly, "I should not have
gone anyhow. And you must not give me so much
credit. There were mamma and Uncle Robert and
Emma, who was very sweet, and —"

"But if the sower planted his seed, and there was
no rain, or no sun, or no soft dew, would it grow and
ripen? You have been a little cheerful sunshine and
a little softening dew, and gone on with the garden-
er's tireless patience, and at last a tiny bud has put
forth. It is the assistance of everything, not any one
particular word or deed."

" But is it not our duty to keep doing just these things for every one ?   Some one is always doing them for us."

" My child, yes.   It is the little outgrowth of the greater love within us, the Divine love speaking in our familiar tongue.   And if we *could* learn that it does not really impoverish us any !   If you break off the top of a plant it sends out two new shoots, and those below are strengthened.   But sometimes the top is so dear to us that we cannot see all the grace and beauty and tenderness that may be evolved at the very next turn."

She smiled a little, raising her clear, beaming eyes to meet the others so grave yet kindly.

" I don't suppose Christ came down to save the world for his own pleasure."

" No," she answered, softly.   " He thought of us."

" And he asks us to think of the brethren."

They stopped at the door.   " Some of the lessons have been almost forgotten," he said, with a smile, " but there is a little remaining."

He went in and gave the invitation to Ada as well, and then left the girls together.

Ada did not look as bright and cheerful as when

she left Cedarwood. But she was very glad to see Kathie, and the parlors wore a cosier aspect than a year ago. There was a bouquet in a small vase that attracted the child's attention.

"Papa brings me home a fresh one every day or two. I never knew that he cared so much about flowers, except to be proud of them when we had them in abundance"; and Ada sighed over the lost treasures.

"What have you been doing?" Kathie asked, presently.

"Nothing much, I am afraid. I can't seem to get to a place where there is any method. Your house is so quiet and orderly that you can hardly understand the lack of system. We have had dreadful times with cooks, and that frets mamma. Then Mary had made up her mind to leave when her month was up, but I do believe I persuaded her out of it."

"You had some influence then."

"It *was* a hard situation. I know I never realized how much I demanded of a girl. It kept her always busy and always behindhand, for there is so much to do. She liked us all, and was very well satisfied, only

15

the work was too hard. So I proposed to keep my room in order and take charge of the parlors, and after we had tried it a few weeks she was content to stay."

Kathie smiled a quick approval.

"But I get so tired at times. I believe I do not like to work, and it seems the same old thing over and over. I wish I had Miss Lauriston's gift for painting, I would study at once. I have tried a little, but I have no especial genius, that is clear."

"And the music?"

"There are so many really good singers that it does not seem of much account, unless one wished to teach or to go on the stage. I don't suppose I ever could be a *prima donna.* So I play now and then for papa, o to keep the boys still. You would hardly believe that I have been learning some of the street songs to please them."

"I am sure that is of some account," Kathie said, warmly.

"But those are all such trifles."

"And the trifles make the larger things."

"You are a born philosopher, Kathie," Ada returned, laughingly. "I have not so much grace or patience. Come up stairs to my room, for I have been trying to keep Florence out of harm's way until Mary has the nursery in order."

Florence had a dozen dolls of different sizes spread out on the floor, and a miniature Saratoga wardrobe scattered around.

"O Florrie! what a place you have made!" Ada exclaimed. "I said you must keep in this corner."

"But it crowded me so much. And I was packing up to go to the seaside. O, it is Miss Kathie!"

Florence made one spring to Kathie's arms.

"O Florence, you are so boisterous, like a great boy! I wonder how Lisa used to make them behave so nicely! It seems to me that no one can keep them in order now. No, you cannot sit in Kathie's lap until you have gathered up all those things."

"I won't do it!" said Florence, defiantly.

Kathie unclosed the dimpled arms that were clasping her so fondly, and turned away with a sorrowful expression.

"They don't hurt anybody"; looking very complacently at the disorder.

"Florence, you shall go down stairs!" exclaimed Ada.

"No matter." Kathie turned away and seated herself by the window, the corner of the bureau shutting her off from the child, who appeared dismayed at the sudden move.

"You don't love me any more," she said, with cunning pathos.

"No one loves naughty little girls."

"But I was not naughty to you."

Kathie could hardly forbear smiling. "I am going to talk to Ada until you pick up the dollies' clothes," she returned, in a quiet tone.

"Tell me about Emma and Mr. Langdon," Ada said, resuming her seat. "I feel so much interested in them. When are they to be married?"

"Just after Christmas, I believe."

"It seems so odd that anything really splendid — for it is that — should come in such a quiet life. There are hundreds of girls who would be delighted to marry a man like Mr. Langdon."

Kathie did not doubt it, though to her it appeared the most natural thing in the world. How could any one help loving Emma!

"I have been trying to sew a little, and learning how really ignorant I am in any kind of useful

knowledge. I have done all my mending since I
came home, and when we had a seamstress here I
endeavored to glean a bit or two of useful informa-
tion. And, Kathie, I believe I shall ask papa to give
me an allowance for clothes, and try to make the
most of it. Did you hear Uncle Edward say they
were prospering wonderfully in their business?"

" No, but I am very glad."

" Yet if he should be rich again, I hope not to be
quite so foolish"; and Ada sighed. " I do believe
Aunt Jessie lives a very happy, useful life, and
enjoys a great deal more than mamma. Everybody
likes her so much too. You know I did not admire
her at all at first."

Kathie remembered.

Florence crowded her sunny head in the corner.

"They is all picked up," she announced, softly.

" They *are*," corrected Ada, half tempted to send
her away. But Kathie held her on her lap and talked
with as much interest as if the child made no demands. Ada watched and wondered. How could
she be so charming to everybody? Did nothing
ever fret or annoy?

CHAPTER XIII.

AUNT RUTH IN THE CIRCLE.

THEY were summoned to lunch presently, and then took a promenade on Broadway to see some pictures. Ada had learned one lesson, — to think a little of her guest, and not all of herself. In one gallery she met an old friend, who was exceedingly cordial.

"Mrs. Arde came to call upon us again this fall, and asked me to go out driving with her. I could not help but think of what your mother said, that in adversity we sometimes desert our friends instead of their deserting us. I was ungracious to Mrs. Arde last winter, and it was very kind in her to give me another opportunity. We have commenced to read Italian together, and I go there twice a week. She has a lovely home, and is a thoroughly cultivated woman."

"A friend truly worth having"; and Kathie smiled.

"I think so now. She admires Aunt Jessie very much, and is more of her kind."

Ada went in to make a little call upon the baby, and said good by to Kathie, who was rather tired, and glad to sit down and rest.

Monday morning she went shopping with Uncle Robert. It quite reminded her of the first time she had come to New York. Mrs. Alston had made out a list of articles to be purchased, and they had a good deal of amusement in hunting them up. They did not get through until it was time to go to Dr. Markham's, so he left her at the door, as he had some business on hand with Mr. Meredith.

A very delightful surprise awaited Kathie. Her old friend Mrs. Havens was in town making a visit, and had spent the day with Mrs. Markham. Kathie had grown so much that she declared she hardly knew her, and they had to talk over the excursion down Guilford River, and how the boys were lost in the woods. She had not seen Aunt Ruth at all since her marriage, and was pleased with all the tidings from her.

It was quite late when Dr. Markham came in, and he was accompanied by a young medical friend whom he introduced as Dr. Garnier, — a fine-looking fellow of thirty or thereabouts, who seemed not at all

abashed by the presence of two young ladies, but
handed them both in to supper with a good deal
of politeness. Kathie was a trifle shy, but Ada had
lost neither her art of, nor her desire to, please
gentlemen.

They had a really charming evening. About nine
Uncle Robert came in for Kathie, and as Dr. Garnier
was going too, he begged the privilege of seeing Ada
home. The girls were to meet the next day at the
christening.

A quiet family party, with no great show or lav-
ish expense. Master Robbie acquitted himself very
sweetly indeed, and gained many commendations.

"He is on his good behavior before Kathie," Mr.
Meredith said, mischievously. "I do believe he is
wondering in his queer little brain if he cannot be-
guile her Fortunatus purse from her when he grows
a few years older."

"But he would have to take Uncle Robert too."

"Why, he has him already"; and Mr. Meredith
lifted his eyebrows in surprise. "I expect him to
be a most dutiful nephew. You will not be able to
crowd him out of the circle, Miss Kathie."

Kathie laughingly declared that she had no desire
so to do.

" I am so sorry the visit has come to an end," said Ada, putting on her hat with its drooping brown plume, and looking very stylish. " I get so discouraged thinking out all the puzzles alone, and life *does* seem dreary and barren."

"There is something better than any mere human help," she whispered, softly, — " One who is always ready to listen."

Ada colored. She was so little used to going to the grand Fountain-head for strength.

" It appears almost like a month," said Kathie, on their homeward way. " So many events have been crowded into the few days."

She took up her lessons in good earnest. There was no break until Christmas, which fell on Monday this year. Friday it snowed all day. They were expecting General and Mrs. Mackenzie, but the night closed in without them. Jessie and her husband had come home for a holiday visit, and brought the wonderful boy.

Kathie and Uncle Robert drove over to the station on Saturday, after paying their respects to Robert the Third, as Freddy called him. She ran eagerly through the waiting-room when the train stopped. Yes, there was a sweet, smiling face, and the other graver and older, but none the less happy.

"Dear, dear Aunt Ruth!"

Kathie would never outgrow any of the old loves. In her warm and constant heart they would be as fresh years hence as in her most demonstrative childhood.

"How good it seems to get home once more!" Aunt Ruth exclaimed. "For, after all, there is no place with quite the same memories as Brookside."

Kathie squeezed her hand fondly.

"But you had a nice time out at the fort," she said. "Rob thought it splendid."

"I have had 'nice times,' as you call it, everywhere. I have been very happy, but it does not render the old home less dear or beautiful."

"Some day I hope we shall have one of our own," General Mackenzie exclaimed. "I am growing rather tired of this wandering life."

Kathie thought of Bruce's secret and laughed softly to herself. What was there in it that required such sacred keeping? Very likely she would know all about it sooner than he, but she made no comment.

This Christmas would still be a little different from

all that had gone before. There were to be no guests
at all, and, to Freddy's great disappointment, no
Christmas-tree; but then he had invitations to half
a dozen others. Each of the Sunday-schools in the
village had requested generous contributions, and
were planning to have quite a gala time. Then the
Morrisons had a "beauty," and several of Freddy's
schoolmates had begged him to be sure and come.

Kathie had been very busy with her gifts, striving
to remember all who needed love or help. Each year
she arrived at a clearer understanding of these duties
and claims, and it became a deeper pleasure to per-
form them. God had given her all things richly to
enjoy, but not for self-aggrandizement. Like the
loaves and the fishes, and the supper of the king,
there were others to be called in and fed. The germ
of enjoyment was to widen until it embraced the
multitude, even those of the highways and byways.

And here Mrs. Alston's judicious hand guided and
restrained. There were gifts of use and beauty. She
possessed the rare art of ministering to souls as well
as to bodies. There were homes in which a book, a
vase, or a simple picture gave the keenest pleasure,
because these people felt they had no money for lux-

uries. Necessities they must have, — food and rai-
ment, — but the bits of delight that gladden the
heart like a stray gleam of sunshine were doubly
prized from the hand of another.

Aunt Ruth was quite fatigued with her long journey, taken in haste as it had been. She looked so
natural in the " crimson room," which for all its use
had not grown shabby. There was the window full
of flowers and trailing vines, tended mostly now by
Uncle Robert's hand, since there were so many claims
upon Kathie.

Aunt Ruth lay on the lounge in the Sunday evening twilight, with Kathie for company. Out of doors
a white moon was shining over the whiter snow,
broken here and there by the clumps of evergreens.
A wonderful night indeed, in its awe and mystery, as
if the heavens might open and the Son of God come
down again to be born anew for sinful men. Kathie
seemed to feel it all as she drew nearer to Aunt Ruth
and clasped the soft hand.

" It always appears like the beginning of a new life
when we come to any such event," she said, slowly.

"A pleasant starting-point. Something to give us
hope and courage, and to remind us that small begin-

nings may lead to glorious results. It did not seem eighteen hundred years ago as if the world could be redeemed by a simple babe being born into it, and that the work would go on each year gathering force and strength, until every nation and clime sends forth men to worship him."

Kathie knelt in a little awe and laid her cheek beside the other.

" Dear Aunt Ruth," she said. " I used to wonder *how* we followed him, and how we could do things for his glory. But with every step the way becomes clearer."

" 'He that doeth my will shall know of the doctrine.' It is the work, after all, that enlightens us. When we take one step, the way becomes plainer for the next."

Kathie understood that too. The mysteries that used to puzzle her had rolled away like the gray clouds in a morning sunrise. Then she smiled with a sweet quaintness.

" Well ?" Aunt Ruth said, studying the pure, changeful face.

" I was thinking about the old times, and when I first began to care about these things. At first it was to please mamma."

"As if all true human love was not a type of the Divine. 'He prayeth best who loveth best.'"

"Yes, I tried because I loved her and was sorry for her hard life. And it seems only yesterday that I sat and read my fairy-book until it was dark, and forgot that she wanted me to do errands. And how little we all were! When I pass the old cottage I wonder if we did actually live there, and were poor and sad, and if Uncle Robert came home. It seems as if we must have had him always."

"I suppose it is quite difficult for you to make anything more than a dream out of the past. My darling, I am glad the good fortune came while you were so young. I think you will learn to use it wisely, and feel that it is one of God's choicest earthly gifts, that need not crowd one out of heaven in the end."

"God has been very good to us," she said, reverently.

General Mackenzie entered the room softly, and crossed over to them.

"Are you keeping a Christmas vigil?" he asked. "May I share it with you?"

"Not exactly a vigil. Giving thanks, rather, for the past joys."

"It is good to count them up on this night of all nights. I, too, have many to remember."

They talked them over in the waning light, and they were not half told when the darkness fell like a mantle, for the young moon had dropped out of sight in the bosom of the clouds. But they had all been very near each other's hearts.

"It will be a hard day for you, Freddy," his mother said, at the breakfast-table. the next morning. "And if you go to your party to-night you must not tire yourself out."

The party was a great event. It was at the house of one of his schoolmates. The "tree" was to be at eight precisely, with plays and music and a supper.

"It is rather a pity that some of them cannot begin in the morning," Uncle Robert said, smilingly. "The earliest is at three, I believe."

Freddy was in a state of supreme exaltation. He had at last become the owner of a pretty silver watch in a hunting-case. It was a sore temptation to wind it up about every five minutes, for it seemed as if it must run down or something happen to it.

Kathie had not been forgotten. General Mackenzie had brought her a beautiful chromo, which was not unveiled to curious eyes until Christmas morning. And here was a set of the poems she loved, and stray books for which she had expressed a longing.

"I began to think there was nothing else for me to have," she said, archly.

"Did you suppose that you had gone to the end of pleasures so soon?" asked Uncle Robert.

"No, I can never do that"; and her soft eyes were lustrous with emotion.

A lovely day with a crisp, fresh air, not too cold for sleigh-riding, and the whole world seemed musical with the undertone of bells. They all went to church in the morning, and then had a quiet dinner. It was so good to have Aunt Ruth once more that Kathie almost dreaded the advent of any one. There were so many dear old events to talk over.

She only went down to the Morrisons' to light their tree and witness the children's joy. Ethel's father had come back for a brief visit. He was doing very well indeed, and thought another year he might venture to take his little daughter out with him.

Fred came home from every tree laden with spoils. His mother felt quite sure that he would make himself sick eating so many cakes and candies, and be-

sought him to save his appetite for the party. At
last he began his grand dressing operations, but came
to a dead halt about his neck-ribbon. What color
did Aunt Ruth think the prettiest? Kathie was sure
to say blue, but he wore blue to school and everywhere.

" I think I have a pretty lavender one," said Aunt
Ruth.

She found it, and tied it to perfection. Kathie
scented his handkerchief with her " Kiss me quick,"
and gave him a fond kiss herself.

" Why, it is almost like the time you went to a
party," exclaimed Freddy, " ever and ever so long ago
in a blue silk dress."

Kathie laughed merrily. She could never forget
that Cinderella episode.

" But you are grander still," she answered. " I
did not have any Uncle Robert, nor any ponies and
sleigh."

Mr. Meredith and Jessie were over a little while
in the evening. Kathie felt that it had been a very
happy day, if a quiet one. Her heart seemed full
to overflowing.

Fred's party was a brilliant success. Several little

16

girls kissed him for the prettiest, and he danced in
every set. His head ached a little the next morning,
and he did not want any breakfast, but by noon he
was out snowballing, as merry as a cricket.

Kathie went over to Emma's on Tuesday afternoon
and stayed all night with her. She had wanted Kathie for her bridesmaid at first, but this had not been
deemed advisable, so Sue Coleman was to stand
instead, with a friend of Mr. Langdon. Kathie took
her pretty gift with her. There would be no display
of bridal presents, or, indeed, of any kind. A simple
marriage in church with a few friends present, and a
serious taking up of the new life before them. Yet
Emma was very happy with the tender joy of love
and trust. During her brief engagement she had
grown into her lover's heart to be a part of himself.
Somewhere their lives had touched and assimilated,
and they were not the lives to stray off again into
tangled or hidden paths.

There was a larger concourse than they had expected. Emma was in an exquisitely becoming trav-
elling-dress, and the long plume in her hat drooped
over her soft hair like a spray of showering mist.
Much fashion had not been called upon to lend its

aid, yet she looked more truly beautiful and bride-like than if overloaded with laces and ribbons, though Sue declared afterward that it was a pity it could not have been a full-dress wedding with such a handsome couple.

The Alstons and several others rode to the station to see them off.

"It is just the kind of a marriage to give one new faith," General Mackenzie said. "It was like a quaint old English picture. You could see love and reverence and trust in both faces, in every gesture and word. Mr. Langdon is be commended for choosing the pure gold when the world is so full of dross."

Kathie did not care to talk any that evening. Every week it appeared as if life deepened and widened. There was a sweet awe and tenderness in it that she had never known before, mingled, too, with a reverent humility. Friends came in and brought their sweetness, which lingered like the scent of lavender and rosemary in some old drawer, and would never fade wholly away.

"It is always hard to go back to school after a holiday," she said the next week. "But there is one comfort, Aunt Ruth, you will not disappear in a trice

It will be very charming to come home of an afternoon and find your sweet face in this familiar room."

No, Aunt Ruth did not mean to disappear in a hurry. General Mackenzie went down to New York and stayed a night or two, and was even recalled to Washington for a week, but Aunt Ruth remained at Cedarwood. She and Kathie enjoyed each other's society as much as in the sick-room at Dr. Markham's, perhaps more, for now there were journeys and people to talk about, and many subjects that Kathie was just coming to understand.

Emma was a month away, and in that time a new world had been opened to her. Mr. Langdon had enjoyed the exquisite delight of bringing rich stores to her appreciative mind, and reading the guileless soul, so different from the worldly, hackneyed ones too often met. He had indeed won a prize, and perhaps he understood still better than she where the child Kathie's influence had unconsciously given her strength.

"If Ada was only as happy as everybody else I should feel quite well satisfied," Kathie would say to Aunt Ruth.

Ada's record appeared to be a troublous one indeed. She wrote to Kathie with tolerable fairness. She had

seen the true way, she had known by brief glimpses
of that higher and more satisfying life, and yet it was
hard to walk therein. She realized daily that it was
difficult to serve God and mammon.

Mrs. Meredith had made another plunge into gay
society, — for Ada's sake, she said. It would not do
to let her daughter's best years pass by with no attempt to regain what they had lost. Ada was really
prettier than she had ever been, and her health so
fully re-established that a fashionable season could
be very well endured. They were more prosperous,
and though it was not possible to indulge in the old
style and luxuries, they could have some society at
least. The Meredith name had not lost all its pres-
tige. Now that the world saw a probability of Mr.
Meredith once more becoming a wealthy man, it
hasted to do them honor.

So there were late nights of dissipation, dancing in
hot, crowded rooms, suppers when the system was
weary and relaxed, the excitement of dressing, the
temptation to " envy, hatred, malice, and all unchar-
itableness." For Ada's eyes were clearer now. She
could see the pretence and hollowness, the captious,
critical spirit that tore one's best friends into shreds,

that was fair to one's face and full of deceit in one's
absence.   And the great aim of all the weakness, sin,
and folly was a good marriage.

Even here she found that her ideas had undergone
a great change.   Truth and honor and manliness on
the one side, with purity and reverence on the other,
were becoming indispensable.   The men she had been
studying lately were nobler in mind than the vapid
butterflies of fashion, or middle-aged exquisites who
tried to counterfeit the semblance of youth without
its freshness and natural grace.

She did try to keep her heart and mind from
being again entangled in this rubbish.   Mrs. Arde
proved a true and valuable friend, and Uncle Edward
was always ready to cheer and sustain with the tenderest love.   But the late nights brought the usual
result of weary mornings, when she felt depressed,
feverish, overstrained in every nerve, and absolutely
fretful.   The old disorder began to creep into her
room.   Florence said, with a grave shake of her head,
"I don't love you any more, 'cause you are cross
to me."

Sometimes she wondered if there was any use in
trying.   It was very well for Kathie in her simple

home, with everything to help her, but could *she*
make any headway? Was it not useless striving?
And perhaps, in her moments of despondency, she
would have given up and drifted with the tide but
for her father. Without precisely understanding the
difficulties in her way, he bridged many of them over
by his tender love. Now and then a quiet evening
with him refreshed and strengthened her, and af-
forded him so much pleasure that she felt amply
repaid. But it was hard work to serve two masters,
and not even Kathie guessed the many failures
and discouragements. Although Dr. Markham was
"queer," he discerned the struggle more readily than
any one, and steered her now and then through rapids
and over shoals. For so it is in this life that one
planteth and another gathereth the fruit.

Mrs. Alston and her brother were driving homeward one morning after numerous calls, the last of
which had been at the post-office. He opened his
letter from Rob carelessly, but after he had read
half a dozen lines his brow was crossed by a little
perplexity.

"Some trouble again!" Mrs. Alston exclaimed, ap-
prehensively. "No mischief, I hope, nor disgrace?"

"No, set your heart at rest. Nothing of much importance, and it can be easily remedied."

She could not be satisfied with the answer, however. After a silence of some minutes, she said, in a low, sad tone, "What is it, Robert? His mother surely has a right to know."

"He has foolishly run in debt again."

"And we thought him going on so well. Will there never come an end to the anxiety about him? It seems to me that he might learn."

"My dear Dora, he has his whole lifetime for the purpose. We must not abridge the liberal allowance God has made, to have it conform to our narrow ideas."

"Are you not too indulgent?"

Mr. Conover smiled thoughtfully. "I rather expected it," he said. "It would be strange if he passed all temptations, with his impulsive nature and want of thought. He has gone through the best part of his year with only this grave error, so we must excuse him. And I like the manner in which he writes about it."

"How much is it?"

"Only forty dollars now. Let me read you this.

" ' I want to come to confession in Kathie's fashion, dear Uncle Robert, sorry indeed that I have gone astray, and needing a little help to extricate me from trouble. I have been foolish and gone in debt again. The first was about the holidays. Half the class gave a little supper, and, not supposing it would be very expensive, I joined. We had a gay, jolly time, but the bills amazed us all. One of the fellows loaned me some money, and I thought I could soon pay it back. That took me into the set, and somehow there has been one thing and another, and the treating that I thought I was cured of, until I have gone behindhand every month. In a week I must pay twenty dollars, and I have n't anything at all towards it. I have tried to save and to pay, but I seem to be getting deeper all the time. I have resolved solemnly, however, that I *will* break with the set, for there are the temptations of drinking, smoking, and gambling; and, if one does n't do much at it, the money goes before one thinks. But I have not smoked a cigar nor touched a drop of liquor since I have been here. I have been tempted a good many times, but I thought of my promise to you, which, God helping me, I mean to keep. And now I am going to get out of this set and stay out, so I don't want to ask any more favors of them. Will you please advance me the money and take it out of my allowance afterward ?   It was the only way I saw out of the difficulty, and I thought I would summon courage enough to tell you the whole truth.   I did mean to be so good and trustworthy too ; but it seems as if I was always getting into some trouble.   Dear Uncle Robert, have you any faith left in me ?'

"You see he discovered the best way out, and that is something.   I like his frankness."

"But how could he have gone so in debt ? "

"I merely allowed him enough for comforts, not luxuries, and he has been indulging in them.   We will make this all straight, however, and let him take a fair start."

"His lessons have to be learned over many times."

"Is it not so with the most of us until we follow the true light that never leads men astray ?   It will dawn for him some time."

Mrs. Alston sighed, and breathed a prayer for her first-born.

CHAPTER XIV.

BRINGING IN THEIR SHEAVES.

MRS. WILDER'S rooms were filled with visitors again. It was quite as much to go to her examination as to the Academy. A number of last year's pupils were there as well, though the graduating class was not as large this summer.

Kathie had been studying very diligently for the last three months, anxious to have school-life close for her. Not that she expected to drop everything then and sink into idleness. Each year she understood better the value of knowledge, and the many duties life held for her. But change is always sweet to youth.

They were warmly congratulated on their success. Emma, and Sue, and a bevy of girls, hovered about Kathie.

" I am so glad it is over. I feel free as a bird "; and the sweet face was full of smiles and dimples.

" And you will get dreadfully bored before another

year has ended," exclaimed Sue. "I am so tired of
myself sometimes that I have half a mind to set up
school-teaching in sheer self-defence."

Tired of one's self and freedom! Why, it was the
loveliest thing in the world!

"And now you are going to West Point. You *are*
a lucky girl. One cannot help envying you."

Yet how many changes and pleasures Sue Coleman
had! Kathie could not understand the spirit of un-
rest and dissatisfaction.

"Yes. We shall be in time for the very last. I
am sorry we could not go sooner."

"And you will bring Cadet Mackenzie home with
you. Is he going in the army?"

"I suppose so, of course."

"Well, do give us a chance to see him. He is a
cousin, so you need not be afraid."

"Afraid of what?"

Two or three of the girls laughed, and Kathie's
cheeks were scarlet.

Mrs. Wilder stopped her to have a few last words.
"We have taken a great deal of pleasure together,"
she said, "and I am honestly sorry to lose you. Your
courage and truth and sweetness have comforted me

many a time when I felt half discouraged, and I can see more plainly than any one else what good service it has done in the school. I wish there were more girls like you. And now, though I lose my pupil, I hope always to keep a sunny-hearted girl-friend. You will be able to find an occasional hour for me."

"Indeed I shall," Kathie returned, warmly, her face full of radiant blushes at the unlooked-for commendation. What had she done that should bear fruit so manifold?

There were kisses and partings, promises to call and to visit, and the confusion of a general dispersion. When Kathie reached home she was absolutely tired out. She and Aunt Ruth had some lunch together.

"Now you must lie down and rest," Aunt Ruth said; "for we must be up early to-morrow, and it will be a tiresome day."

"But I feel as if I could n't keep still," Kathie returned. "I am all in a flutter."

"Nervous excitement, which a little rest will allay. I will sit and read to you, which will divide your thoughts and tranquillize you."

"Let it be 'Songs of Seven' then."

Kathie listened dreamily to the sweet voice making melody with the poet's meanings. She, too, had said her lesson " over and over."

General Mackenzie was awaiting them in New York. He was deeply interested in his son's examination, and had been up nearly every day. So they started the next morning, and, as they had to wait but an hour for the train, took a little lunch without calling upon anybody. And by night they were making themselves comfortable at the hotel.

It was glorious weather. Nature was out in her holiday array. The parlor, the long promenades, and the Academy grounds were brilliant with flitting figures of parents, friends, and stray visitors for pleasure's sake merely. Young cadets went smiling about, and there was no lack of older military men. Kathie thought it an endless procession of strange faces. And how gay they were!

Then there were the beautiful parades and drills and evolutions, the invitations to dinners, suppers, hops, and all manner of festivities.

"Aunt Ruth and I have concluded that to pity poor cadets for their hard time is a sheer waste of sympathy," Kathie said, laughingly, to Bruce.

"O, it is not all like this, you need not imagine. This is a sort of summer glorifying, when sisters and cousins and sweethearts smile upon us like June roses. There is many a week when it is dull enough."

"It seems like a daily festival, with all the music and parades and beautiful dressing. I wonder that you do not forget your important points for examination."

"I am nearly through mine, and glad enough I shall be. I feel as if I had been on the rack for the past fortnight, and my brain has been so stretched and twisted and tortured that presently there will be a fearful collapse. Pity me when you hear the report."

"Shall you lose your senses?"

"And become an idiot? I hope not. I want to enjoy all that may happen after this trying time"; and he gave her an odd smile. "But I am so glad you came. I counted every day."

She smiled too, and colored a little.

"I can sympathize with you, as I have just been passing the dreaded ordeal," she said, in mock condolence.

"And very successfully too, I heard. I must be careful not to shame you. But O, won't there be one immense thanksgiving when the matter has been brought to a triumphant conclusion! Then there are all the years of service."

"But you are not to enter immediately."

"No. It is my debt of honor, though. And I shall be proud to follow my father's footsteps."

There could be little doubt of that, Kathie thought, as she glanced at the manly figure, lithe yet rounded, supple, and graceful. How imperceptibly the boy had changed into the man! And how strange to be as familiar with him as with Rob or Charlie!

At last came the final tug, but Bruce, like a good soldier, had his forces all in light marching order. No tripping up, or stammering, or having an idea slip out of one's mind just when it was most needed. As Kathie said afterward to Rob, it was really magnificent.

General Mackenzie was congratulated upon his promising son, and well might he be proud of him. Essentially truthful, honest, and noble, perfect in health, and possessing not a few attributes of manly beauty. What more could one ask?

They remained for a grand supper and ball, though Aunt Ruth declared that Kathie must go as the simplest of wild flowers, since they had not counted upon so much gayety. But she looked as pretty in her sheer white muslin as the others in tarletan and silk, and enjoyed the dancing quite as well. Indeed, several of the cadets rather envied Bruce his cousin.

They came down to New York on the boat. It was a very lovely sail, and Bruce kept her interested by descriptions and legends of sundry places that they passed. To Kathie it appeared almost like an enchanted country. After a while they lapsed into silence. It was so unutterably beautiful, with the cloudless sky overhead, and the broad, rippling river, with its banks of green foliage or gray rock tangled about with moss and vines. Here and there a nook where fairies might dwell in safety, or a vista among the opening trees that appeared to lead to another world.

" I sometimes wonder if Italy can be any lovelier," Kathie said, slowly.

Bruce glanced up with a peculiar expression. "Would you like to see it ? " he asked.

" O, what a question ! As if any one could refuse.

17

But I don't suppose I ever shall. So many delightful things happen to me continually that I must not be selfish enough to want everything."

He laughed softly. "But if it should really be possible — "

She gave him a quick, questioning look.

You know I told you last year that I had a secret, a very sweet one, that I could hardly keep to myself. But I have permission to tell you now, — I begged so to be the first. We are all going abroad."

" All ? " she said, bewildered.

" Yes. Father, mother, you and I, and perhaps Mr. and Mrs. Edward Meredith.

" Oh ! " in a soft tone of incredulity, for she could not believe a word of it.

" Yes. Father had an offer to go to Europe on some governmental business, but he decided to wait until I could accompany him. We are to go to Russia first, but we shall visit everything worth seeing before we return."

" But I — "

" It was my idea, — out at the fort "; and a rosy hue suffused his face. " Father took it up instantly, but nothing was to be said then. Mother settled it

all with Mrs. Alston when she first came back from
the West."

"It is too good!" Kathie said, falteringly, and turned
away her face. "And so — strange."

"But you *will* like it?" He was in an agony of
boyish apprehension lest some other feeling might
interfere.

"Like it? As if —

Her voice seemed to melt away in the murmur of
the waters. It was quite impossible to realize it
at first, and so thoroughly enchanting that she could
not even think two straight, consecutive thoughts
about it.

"Is it true?" she asked of Aunt Ruth, when she
could get safely under the shelter of her kindly wing.
"Am I really going to Europe with you?"

"Yes, my darling."

"But Uncle Robert — and mamma —"

"Could neither of them leave home at present.
There are Rob and Freddy, you know, and my little
girl cannot have all the mother-love. We have talked
it over ever so many times, and mamma is perfectly
willing to trust you to my care. I suppose it will be
hard doing without Uncle Robert."

"And I never guessed a word! How could you keep it such a secret?"

"O, easily. It was best that you should not know while you had so many other things on your mind. And Bruce counted so upon giving you the first hint."

"I am afraid I was n't joyful enough. But when anything goes down deep in your heart, you cannot talk much about it at first. And will the Merediths go?"

"I think they will. The firm have been taking in a new partner, and now it is necessary for one member to go to Europe, as they mean to enlarge their business. It seems best that this should be Mr. Edward Meredith."

"And dear Jessie. O Aunt Ruth, it is too sweet and good to be true!"

Aunt Ruth smiled.

They were to spend a week in New York, as there was some shopping to be done.

"Though we need not burden ourselves with clothes," Aunt Ruth said. "We can get whatever we want abroad with less trouble than to carry it thither."

Jessie was full of interest and excitement.

"The instant it was proposed I wanted to go," she said, "for the party will be just perfect. We are all of one mind, and we all enjoy the same things, so we need not be afraid of each other. I am so glad to have you counted in, though it is a mystery to me that Uncle Robert consented."

Then they must talk a little of Ada.

"She is really nobler than I gave her credit for," Jessie said. "It is a hard struggle to lead that peculiar life, and her mother has been trying her best to make Ada marry a man unsuitable in every respect, except that he is wealthy. Of course Ada had no regard for him, but how many girls think only of an elegant establishment!"

"She has strength and truth then."

"Yes. She will be a long time in finding the right way, and in having courage to walk in it; but when I heard that, it gave me hope. And Edward was so pleased. I think —"

Jessie made a pause and colored. Kathie questioned her with her eyes.

"It is a little gossip, but I know you will be interested. You met Dr. Garnier last fall?"

"Yes," Kathie replied.

"He is a pet and *protégé* of Dr. Markham. A
splendid fellow, too, with some fortune of his own,
and through uncle's influence getting nicely estab-
lished. The old gentleman would scout the idea of
match-making, but he throws them together pur-
posely, I do believe. And what makes me have
more faith in it is Ada's humility about it. She
thinks him so noble that she would never dare try
for him, but I am quite sure that he will try for her.
He applauded Ada's resolve not to marry for money
or station, and thinks it was dreadful in her mother
to wish her to do it."

Kathie was very glad. She was seeing more of the
world and worldliness, and it had the effect of making her cling the more closely to the simple truth.

Ada rejoiced very thoroughly when she heard the
good news.

"You deserve it, if any one ever did," she said to
Kathie. "Every step of the way will be lovely, and
I shall often dream about you. So I wish you the
best good."

Mr. Meredith was touched by his daughter's rejoic-
ing in the matter. "I don't know but I might let
you go with them," he exclaimed, "only I should hate

to give you up for so long a time. You are becoming my little pleasure and comfort."

"Do not think of it, papa"; and Ada's voice was tremulous. "I know that we ought not afford it, and I am content to stay at home."

"My precious child!"

And as Ada was held to his heart, she felt rewarded indeed. The other pleasure might come some time when she could take it with a clearer conscience.

An hour or two afterward, when Dr. Garnier dropped in, Mr. Meredith had to repeat the episode.

"I am very glad you decided not to go," he said, in his honest, straightforward manner; but an unusual sound in his voice brought the color to Ada's cheek. Was it of any importance to him whether she went or stayed?

Bruce enjoyed himself famously escorting both girls around. He was very gallant and gentlemanly, but confessed privately to Kathie that he got on much better with Ada than formerly.

The shopping was finished at length, and the party returned home. They were to start on the first of August. General Mackenzie went to Washington for a few days, taking Bruce and Rob with him, the latter having just commenced his college vacation. So the ladies had a quiet time sewing.

Kathie's projected tour created quite a sensation. It was the general impression that everything nice *did* happen to her. But no one really envied her, and though they should all miss her very much, they were glad to have her go. One and another dropped in to take tea for the last time, but Mrs. Alston managed that there should be nothing sad about the visits.

Sarah Strong came for a day. No one would have thought of connecting her with the frowzy, uncultured girl who had questioned Kathie at the fair. She had grown much, and was rather above medium size. Not a pretty girl, but with something very sweet and noble in her face, for the soul had shaped it to finer expressions.

"I had to come and tell you the good news," she said. "I was examined before the committee, and did splendidly. They gave me a certificate, and yesterday I received my appointment. I am to have two hundred dollars the first six months, and two hundred and fifty the next. You never saw a prouder man than father. I am to live home all the same,

and I keep thinking how many pretty things I shall
do, and how I can help with the other children. O
Miss Kathie, I owe every bit of it to you!"

"No," returned Kathie; "only a very little."

"Yes, all. I should not have known what I
wanted but for you, and I certainly could not have
told how to go about it. There is such a sweetness
and comfort in knowledge that I want to go on and
on, and open the eyes of others to its blessings as
well. But the first-fruits of the harvest I bring to
you."

Kathie had given of her best, and now it was returned fourfold.

"I want you to write me a letter once in a while,
and I will try to get books to read that will describe
the places you visit, and I will say to myself, 'She is
here now. She is wandering about these beautiful
palaces and picture-galleries, or lakes and mountains,
and enjoying these wonderful sights and scenes.'
Why, it will be almost as good as if I were there
myself!" and Sarah's face glowed with unfeigned
pleasure.

"I can liken it to nothing but harvest days," Kathie said, as she sat alone with Aunt Ruth that even-

ing. "I seem to be gathering up so much love and tenderness, so many good wishes, until my heart is full to overflowing with golden sheaves. And everything drops right into my lap. I did not know that anybody could be so full of joy and happiness."

Aunt Ruth smiled back to the sweet face. Did she know that she was reaping as she had sown, that the fruits of the spirit were joy, peace, and tender content? Very little grains they had been at first, and sown in her own heart, oftentimes choked with weeds and perishing for lack of moisture; but she had remembered, had tried, and God's promises are true. His word never fails.

It is a great deal for a child, you say. Ages ago a little Syrian maid, a captive, — or slave, if you will, — carried away into a strange land, and, no doubt, bowed down with sorrow and loneliness, bethought herself of the work of mercy. Her master was a leper, but she did not say, "He is a heathen, and it makes no difference whether he is healed or not," or, "He may not believe I am telling the truth," but bore testimony in the simplest, sweetest fashion. She knew that her God was all-powerful, and that his prophets could

work his will, so she besought her master to go and
be healed. The result you know. Can we not believe
and do in our own land, in our own homes ?

Mrs. Alston dreaded to spare her child, but she was
not selfish. Bruce could remain abroad only a year,
but the others would stay until they had satisfied
themselves.

Rob could hardly be reconciled. It seemed as if
the whole world were going away. His years of college life looked positively insupportable.

"Not that I envy you, Kathie," he explained ; " but
the nice things do come naturally to you, as if they
always knew their way, and could not make a mistake."

" You had the Western trip last summer, and there
will be a good many pleasures, I know. It is only
waiting a little longer."

" And that is just what is so hard. Then Bruce
and I could have such a splendid time." Rob sighed
forlornly. Besides, when Kathie went, the light of
the house would be gone.

One day they commenced packing. Still it did not
seem a bit real to Kathie, in spite of the good-bys. It
was like the other little journeys she had taken

Only there was a shadow in mamma's face and a tremble in her voice.

"My darling, I hardly know what I shall do without you," she said, "but I can trust you to Aunt Ruth and to yourself. I am thankful this opportunity has occurred, for I am afraid I should never have the courage or energy for years of travel. You will be very happy, I know, and your constant heart cannot stray far from the home-circle. You have given me many happy years and very little sorrow. God bless you and watch over you daily."

Kathie's tears fell silently, but they were not all sorrow.

"I am glad if I have made you happy, mamma," she said, with a soft little sob.

"My darling!" and the mother held her to her heart for many minutes.

"Don't be surprised if we should cross your orbit after the fashion of a comet," Mr. Langdon said, laughingly. "I dare say Emma will be wanting a glimpse of Italy and Paris and the Louvre, and you may stumble over Rob amid Alpine glaciers."

"I wish they might," confessed Rob.

They all went down to New York. Their luggage

was taken on board, their staterooms inspected, and everything pronounced satisfactory. The Markhams came to see them off, Mr. George Meredith, Ada, and Dr. Garnier. It was like a little party, and each one tried to keep the other from being sad.

But by and by the great bell rang. Kathie kissed Uncle Robert dozens of times.

"For you have been and always will be my fairy-prince," she said, through her tears. "If I could take you and mamma it would be perfect."

Sad, sweet, lingering words. Hands clasped and unclasped. Faces averted, slow steps taking them farther and farther, and now the familiar figures were ingulfed in the crowd.

But she saw Rob on the pier waving his handkerchief, mamma and Uncle Robert smiling. Ah, she was not to carry away sorrowful pictures of them! And then the noble ship steamed down the bay. Faces, figures, wharves, houses, steeples, were lost to sight. The Narrows opened before them, and all the level bay was glinted over with sunshine.

"Glorious!" Bruce exclaimed. "It is like a sunset. Farewell, dear old native land. We shall never forget you, even for an hour."

Kathie raised her eyes and smiled through her tears. Here were Aunt Ruth and Jessie and baby Robbie, and the other two who loved her dearly; above, God, who would take care of them all, and bring them back safely.

So, little Kathie, thou mayst glean on other smiling harvest fields. Thou wilt never come back empty-handed.

What else ? You can guess at her pleasures and delights. You will know that they missed her in the dear old home, but that she returned and glorified it. You can think of Rob as daily growing in manliness, honor and strength, now and then making a raid on some giant who has crept in unawares, and beating him out of his lurking-place. Of Freddy, with a less boisterous and troublesome boyhood; of Sarah Strong, doing her duty in her state of life, and exerting a wider influence than shallow Belle Hadden ever dreamed of. Ada, stumbling and wearying, yet holding fast of the faith until a stronger arm and loving, earnest heart shall make the crooked paths straight, and lead her gently therein. Of little Ethel, brightening her father's Western home, and as they sit on the door-step of summer evenings talking of the time

when he worked and suffered in another's stead, and
of dear Miss Kathie. Charlie Darrell, with his face
set Zionward, thinking of the day when he too shall
bring "glad tidings" in God's name. Somehow all
these good and tender impulses seem connected with
Kathie. The child sowed her seed farther than she
knew Brave, sunny-hearted Dick, making a place
in the world. Fred Lauriston, useful and trustworthy. Emma, a happy wife and mother, stealing a
little time now and then for her art.

And Uncle Robert, the kind adviser, the generous
friend, the tender, patient, Christian gentleman, his
heart rich in love and good works, for him there
will be joys and rewards even in this world, and
in the other a thousand fold. To Kathie and Rob he
will always be a Sir Galahad, purest and sweetest of
men. Rob's hero-worship veers around a little, or
else his two models have grown indistinguishably
alike.

The old dream or allegory of Jacob's ladder is the
key to all human living. Step by step, reaching from
earth to heaven. Angels ascending and descending.
Like him we build Bethels out of our sorrows, and
learn to see God

And the Apostle said, "God is not unrighteous, that he will forget your works and labor that proceedeth of love; which love ye have showed for his name's sake."

THE END.